ROSE AND THORNE

A Fairytale in the hood
By. Tyanna

Rose and Thorne

Copyright © 2019 by Tyanna

Published by Tyanna Presents
www.tyannapresents1@gmail.com

Acknowledgments

I'm going to start off by thanking God for giving me this gift and also keeping me focused along the way. I also have to thank all of my lovely readers. Without you guys, I wouldn't have made it this far. Shan, I also wanna thank you for trusting in me from the beginning. Here I am on book #38, and it happens to be my very first independent release. I'm nervous, but with my test readers, Chanta C Gray, Kizzy Gray, Chantel Williams, and Jammie Knight, I know they'll keep me straight.

Finally, I can't forget about my pen sisters that also keep me sane, Elle Kayson, Barbie Scott, Chanique Jones, and T'ann Marie. Thank you so much, ladies; whenever I feel like giving up, y'all are my go-to authors, and y'all get me together every time. Throughout this industry, it's hard-finding genuine people, but it's dope to know there are a few out here.

I also have to mention my baby, Tyanna Presents. Whew, it's been a hard road, but I'm making it. Tyanna Presents consists of five authors, Chantel Williams, Torrie Bryant, Nicole Edmond, Sha'Asia Coston, and TN Jones. These ladies also keep me going. I don't just do this for myself and my readers--I also do this for them. I want you ladies to know I thank you all for trusting me to be your publisher. I know I tell y'all often that I'm proud of y'all, but it doesn't hurt to tell you all again. Thank y'all so much for keeping me going.

Thanks again to everyone who has rocked my cover, shared my link, recommended my books, one clicked, read, and reviewed. You all are very appreciated. I hope you all support and enjoy this new hot release, and please be sure to leave a review...

Synopsis

Rose Sanchez, the daughter of a kingpin whose life is turned upside down after her father suddenly dies, is forced to live amongst her grim stepmother and stepsisters. Rose becomes the epitome of a hopeful slave. That's until, lust at first sight, with one of the most wanted, handsome, bad boys by the name of Thorne, turns her smitten. In spite of her circumstances, Rose seeks everything that is taken from her--further placing her at odds with her stepfamily. Will she have the life she was once accustomed to having? Will she have a blissful union with Thorne?

Thorne Williams thought he had everything his heart desired: an untouchable empire, numerous females, and unlimited "street" resources; that is until Rose unexpectedly enters his life. Not able to take his mind off the unfortunate beauty, Thorne sets himself on a path to free Rose from the company of misery and jealousy. After adding fuel to a blazing fire, Thorne's empire is now at stake. Will Thorne successfully rescue Rose? Is his need for Rose more important than solidifying his empire?

CHAPTER 1

Rose

"Rose Sanchez," being yelled out for me to walk across the stage made me proud. I had been through so much in the past six months. I didn't think I was going to make it this far.

"That's my baby right there... go ahead, baby. Get that diploma!" my daddy screamed from the audience as I walked across the stage. Russel 'Big Russ' Sanchez was known in this city because he ran it. People often wondered why he just didn't have me home schooled, and the answer to that was because he wanted me to be comfortable. See, I had lost my mama six months ago from congested heart failure. The day I lost my mama was the worst day of my life. After that, I was forced to move in with my daddy and his ready-made family.

I was born and raised in Atlanta, Georgia. When I turned five, my parents decided to call it quits. My mama couldn't deal with my daddy still being in the streets. He promised when I was born that he was going to give it all up, but five years later, he was still doing the same shit. He wanted us to move to Jersey where he was from, but my mama wasn't having it. So, for years I would come to Jersey for the summer and some holidays. That was until he got married to the wicked witch of the east, Constance Boyd Sanchez.

After the last couple of students walked across the stage, the principal had to do a speech, and I couldn't wait until she was finished. I was starving, and I knew my daddy was taking all of us out to eat.

My daddy tapping me on the shoulder brought me out of my thoughts. I was so in another world I didn't even notice the speech was over, and everyone was starting to get up.

"Come on, baby girl, where we headed to eat? You know it's ya choice," my daddy said. I wasn't really trying to do anything with them since I didn't care for my stepmother and her stuck-up ass daughters. I really had no other choice unless I wanted to go back home and sit in my room all alone. I didn't have any friends; I was what you called a loner. The only friends I had were the ones I left back in Atlanta where I couldn't wait to get back to. I had graduated at the top of my class, and I got accepted to Spelman College. They had been looking at me when I lived in Atlanta. I was so glad they still wanted me.

"I guess we could do Grand Lux Cafe tonight," I said.

"I hate that damn food. I don't know why you always wanna go there," Eboni, the youngest of my stepsisters, snarled.

"Well, it's my choice, and that's where I wanna go!" I snapped back.

"Come on, Eboni, you do like some stuff from there. I wanna hurry up and get this dinner over with so we can head out to the end of the year party," Essence, her sister, said.

"Where's the party at this year?" my stepmother asked.

"The Mansion in Voorhees, and I heard security gon' be tight this year."

"It just better be, as much extra money I sent in towards class dues," my daddy said.

"I don't even know why you put in extra money when you know Rose isn't going to go."

Constance's ugly ass was right. I didn't fuck with people, so I wasn't interested in attending. I didn't even know why Eboni and Essence were going; they didn't even go to the school anymore. Eboni graduated last year, and Essence graduated three years ago.

"Well, Eboni and Essence usually go, and I was hoping Rose would go to enjoy herself. She graduated top of her class, and she deserves to enjoy herself tonight. So, what do you say, princess; you wanna give it a try?" my daddy beamed with a huge smile on his face.

"I'll think about it over dinner. I may see what it's hitting for."

"Yeah Rose, you really should hang out with us," Essence said, shocking the hell out of me.

Eboni sucked her teeth and rolled her eyes. I knew right then and there she wasn't happy. For some reason, she really hated me. Knowing that me going would piss her off even more, I decided right then and there to go ahead and go.

"Ok...since y'all insist, I'll go," I said with a fake smile on my face. After we all agreed on the dinner plans, we all headed out the door to the cars. I rode with my daddy and Constance while Eboni rode with Essence. We were leaving Cherry Hill East; therefore, we weren't far from the restaurant.

Twenty minutes later, we were pulling up at the restaurant. I could still tell Eboni was in her feelings, but I didn't care. I was going out with them and I was going to try to have a good time. I say try because we never got along. It seemed like the whole time I've been here they've treated me like shit. The only thing that kept us from getting into it was my daddy always coming to save the day. I could tell it annoyed him how soft I was. I knew he didn't want us to fight, but I knew he would appreciate it if I stood up for myself, that way they didn't fuck with me. It was nights I would cry and stay locked in my room wishing that my mama was still living so I could go back home.

"Baby, are you ok?" my daddy asked, bringing me out of my thoughts.

"Yes...just thinking about my mama, that's all. We can go ahead in the restaurant," I said, not wanting to continue this conversation. I jumped out of the back seat and made my way into the restaurant with everyone following suit.

"Hello, welcome to Grand Lux Cafe...How many are in your party?"

"It's five of us," I said to the fine ass greeter.

"Ok...well, you all can follow me, and congratulations," he said with a huge smile on his face. I guess he had taken in my appearance and noticed I still had on my graduation gown.

"Thank you so much," I cooed.

"Hey Justin, I didn't even know that was you," Essence said with a dumb ass smirk on her face.

"Hey Essence...I didn't even notice you. How have you been?" he asked.

"I'm good, just living my best life. We should hook up sometime soon for old time's sake." She flirted right in front of her mother and my father like she had no respect.

"Cool...I'm down, you still have my number, right?"

"Of course, I do," she cooed while sitting at the table. I was so over her and her damn sister. They often did shit like this whenever we went anywhere together. It was like everything was a damn competition with them. I didn't say anything until it was time to order my food. I just sat at the table scrolling on social media looking at pictures of all the graduates waiting for the waitress to come take our order.

****

The party had been in full effect for a good hour or more. I didn't fit in because I didn't really deal with anyone. I had only been living in Jersey for a little while, and I still hadn't opened up to anyone.

"You good, Rose?" Essence asked with two red plastic cups in her hand, giving me one.

"Yeah...I'm fine, but what is this?" I asked while frowning my face. I knew liquor wasn't allowed in here, but Essence had managed to find some.

"Just sip it, Rose. It'll make you feel good," Essence said while laughing. I just looked at her and shook my head at her crazy antics. I took a sip, and to my surprise, it didn't taste too bad.

"Hey y'all...didn't I just see y'all earlier?" The dude from Grand Lux Cafe asked while standing in front of us.

"Hey Justin...I didn't know you were coming out," Essence said while smiling from ear to ear.

"You know I wouldn't have missed this for the world. Plus, my boy CJ graduated this year, so I'm here celebrating with him."

"Damn, CJ just now graduating?" Eboni asked while walking up on us.

"Yup, and he been lookin' for you," Justin said, causing Eboni to smile.

"Well, where he at?" Eboni asked while pulling Justin's hand.

"Wait, where y'all goin'?" I asked.

"We chillin', just sit here and wait until we come back," Essence said while pouring the rest of her drink in my cup.

I was sitting on the chair in a daze, and my head was spinning. I knew I was feeling it because everything was going in circles. This dude named Tyreese that I knew from school was standing in front of me with his boy King.

"Hey Rose...what you doin' sittin' here all alone?" Tyreese asked while sitting next to me while King sat on the other side.

"I'm just chilling," I slurred while giggling.

"Yo, she is turnt, bro," King said while shaking his head.

"Rose...why don't you come chill with me and King until Eb and Essence come back?"

"Come on, let's go." I giggled again, but this time, I was standing up. King grabbed one arm, and Tyreese grabbed the other. The three of us were headed out the door. Tyreese always was cool in school even when all the other boys and girls called me fatty, so I just thought he was being a friend. Once we made it to his car, we all sat on the side talking, and I was of course giggling. The alcohol had me so damn drunk, and the crazy part was, I only had one cup.

"Rose...I know you not goin' in yo daddy's house lit like this?" The question he asked caught me off guard.

"What you mean? I'm not drunk."

"Yeah, if you say so," King chuckled.

"Yeah, you are. If you want to, you can lay in the back seat and sleep a little of the liquor off. I know how Big Russ is, and I wouldn't want him to get upset if you walked in the house like this."

"You really think if I take a little nap, it will help?" I asked.

"Yup...and if you want, King and I will stay right out here smoking this L so we can keep an eye on you," Tyreese said in a sincere tone. I listened to him and King and climbed in the back seat and laid down. My head was still spinning, so I figured he might be right about me taking a little nap.

The feeling of rough hands going up and down my thigh woke me up. I didn't even know I had dozed off. I looked up, and Tyreese was in between my legs. The look he had in his eyes told me that he thought something was about to go down.

"What's going on?" I asked in a frightened tone.

"Nothing that you didn't want to happen. Just chill, ma, and let me make you feel good."

"Tyreese, what are you talking about?"

"Come on, Rose, you know you want this just as much as I want this."

"Tyreese, I swear I don't want anything from you," I said while squirming, trying to get away from him realizing that I didn't have much room to move.

"Rose, if you don't keep still you gon' make me get an attitude, then I'm going to get King to help me hold ya fat ass down. Now keep still." Tyreese grimaced. I looked around the car and noticed his dumb ass had all the windows down, so not giving a fuck, I started screaming at the top of my lungs.

"Please, help me...help me!" I yelled as loud as I could until Tyreese slapped me across my face. By then, I was hoping and praying somebody heard me.

"Man, shut her the fuck up. She's drawing too much attention. Fuck...Cace is on his way over here; you better cover her ass up or something," King said sounding afraid. The minute I heard him say someone was on their way over here, I was thanking God right then and there for saving me. "If you say one word when he comes over here, I'ma kill ya stepsisters."

Tyreese grimaced right before he threw a jacket over me.

"What y'all got goin' on over here?" I heard the dude who I assumed was Cace ask.

"Nothing man, we chillin' just like always. What brings you out tonight?"

"Honor graduated, and she asked me to come out with her, since Thorne was busy, but y'all sure y'all good over here?" Cace asked again.

"Yeah man, we cool," King lied.

Getting scared all over again and hearing like they were about to end their conversation, I just couldn't let shit go down like this. I jumped from under the jacket and dug right in Tyreese's eye.

"You fucking bitch!" he yelled out in anger. While I continued to hit him until he opened the car door and rolled out, the dude, Cace, ran around to the back seat and saw me sitting there in a distraught position. By this time, everyone started to walk over to the car. I was still dressed, but the tears were running down my face, and my naturally curly hair was all over the place.

"Oh, my God...Rose, are you OK?" Honor asked while helping me out of the car. I didn't know her like that, but I remembered her from my chemistry class.

"I'm OK, I just wanna go home," I cried, and she helped me walk over to her car. I didn't wanna stick around to see what happened to King and Tyreese. I just wanted to go home shower and go to bed. Today was supposed to be one of the happiest days of my life.

CHAPTER 2

Thorne

"So, what you been up to today?" I asked Big Russ while sitting across from him at his desk.

"Today was my daughter, Rose's, graduation. She graduated from Cherry Hill East today."

"Yo, my little cousin, Honor, graduated from there as well today. I can't believe ya daughter been livin' with you for months now, and I still haven't met her."

"You know how I feel about her. I would keep her hidden away from the world if I could. She did go to that party with Eboni and Essence tonight."

"You really let her go outside with them hot asses?"

"Chill youngin'...don't talk about my stepdaughters like that."

"Well, you know I keeps it real, and I always put you up on what them little thots be into. Now what's up, what's the real reason you called me here?" I asked curious.

"I wanted us to talk about your future plans in the business. In the event that I'm not around much longer, I want you to be prepared for all of this."

"Russ, what the hell you talking about? I hate when you be talking like you ready to leave this earth. You got some time left in you, big homie," I assured him.

"Come on now, Thorne, I want to make sure that you got this shit straight in my absence."

"Russ, you know I got this. You taught me everything I know. I just don't think them old heads that been down from day one gon' like it. They gon' feel some type of way taking orders from a youngin'."

"I don't give a fuck how they feel. I worked too hard to keep my shit up and running without it falling apart, so I'll be damned if the shit falls apart when I leave this earth. They both gettin' too old. Shit, if I was you, I would probably give them both a nice severance pay and let them go," Russ said with a serious look on his face. I couldn't do shit but laugh.

"I swear you are hell, boss."

"You know I am, but that's all I wanted you for, was to make sure you were ready to take over."

"I told you I got it, but you ain't goin' nowhere no time soon, so we should be finished talking about this. I know the passcodes to everything. I know the banks you use. I know all the connects. I got this, big homie, now let me go; I'm meeting up with Kreesha."

"Alright...make sure you strap up and call me tomorrow," Russ said as I got up to walk out. That old man was doing the most, and I didn't understand why. I'd been nickel and diming for Russ since I was fifteen, now I was twenty-four. I had gotten tired of seeing my mama struggling to take care of me, but then she took in my little cousin Honor when my aunt passed, I definitely had to find a way. She hated that I turned to the streets, but she also knew I wasn't going to see her struggle all her life. I jumped up, dapped Russ up, and pulled him in for a one arm hug. I then shot Kreesha a text and jumped in my whip then peeled off.

Ten minutes went by, and Kreesha was already standing in the doorway waiting on me. Kreesha and I had been fucking for a little over five months. She wanna settle down, and I wasn't that dude. I didn't have time for no relationship shit.

"What's good, ma? Why you standin' in the doorway like that?"

"I was waiting for you. What took you so long?"

"I'm here now, so don't worry about all of that. Get me a drink and meet me in the room," I demanded while making my way to her room. Kreesha's house was always clean, and she kept herself together. My issue with her was she was a nagging ass. She drove me crazy with the nagging shit, and we weren't even a couple, so I knew right then and there we could never be. Kreesha was a spoiled brat, and her parents had everything to do with that. She worked at the TD Bank that was in Cherry Hill three days a week, and she also went to Camden County College.

"Mmm... I see you didn't waste no time coming out of them clothes," Kreesha cooed.

"Nope...we already know why I'm here. Come here and give me a hug," I demanded, and she walked over to me seductively with my cup in her hand. I grabbed the cup from her and sat it on the nightstand then pulled her in for a hug. I planted my nose right in the crook of her neck enjoying her scent. It had been a week since I last saw her, and I was ready for whatever the night brought.

"You staying the night with me?"

"Yup... Now let me help you out of this little nightie. I want you ass naked, baby." While I started removing her silk nightie, I began to place soft kisses down her neck. Kreesha rolled her head back enjoying me touching her soft skin. Once I got her nightie off, I pinched each of her nipples right before I leaned down to suck on each one, causing Kreesha to get turned on. She moaned out softly causing me to want her right at this very moment. I threw her on the bed then climbed on top of her. My dick was poking at her opening, but I wouldn't dare go in without having a condom on. I reached over and opened up her nightstand drawer to grab one out of the box that I kept at her house. I then ripped the pack open with my teeth then placed it on the head of my dick. I then placed Kreesha's hand down there to let her finish putting it on for me.

"Oh, you want me to handle that for you?"

"Yeah, rub it on nice and slow, baby." I beamed while she did as she was told. Once the condom was on, I eased nice and slow in her treasure, and her walls instantly began to grab my dick. Her wet, warm, tight insides had me giving her the business. I was so glad I put this condom on because I knew tonight was going to be one of them nights.

We had been doing the damn thing for what seemed like forever, but I still wasn't ready to bust. I wanted to literally be up in her for the rest of the night.

"Turn that ass over, Kree."

She wasted no time doing what I asked. Kreesha tooted that ass in the air, and I got right behind her. I tapped my hard erection on each ass cheek before I entered her.

"This how you want me, zaddy?" Kreesha cooed, making my dick brick up another inch.

"Yup, I want you just like that sexy," I said while stepping back and admiring all this ass I was about to tear up. I drilled in and out of her wetness enjoying every bit of our session.

"Damn girl...keep on throwing that thing back!" I beamed.

"Mmm...you like that, don't you? How about you lay down and let me get on top?"

Kreesha didn't have to tell me twice. I laid down, and she straddled me. Then she slid down on my dick. The feeling of her wetness gripping my dick had my body in overdrive. I started pinching her nipples making her eyes roll back in her head. I could tell she was enjoying the feeling from the faces she was making.

"Fuck...Thorne, I'm cummin', baby," Kreesha said while kissing my lips.

"I am too, beautiful!" I beamed while squeezing both her soft ass cheeks.

After we both came, we laid there getting ourselves together. Once we were both good, I pulled her close to me, and we both drifted off to sleep.

****

The sun shining through the window woke me up from my deep slumber. I looked to my right, and Kreesha was still knocked out. After last night, I knew she would be. Hell, I didn't know why my ass was up already. My phone ringing on the nightstand brought me out of my thoughts. When I grabbed it, I noticed it was Cace, and he had called me at least eleven times.

"What's good, bro?"

"I need you to come to the warehouse right now."

"Why, what happened?"

"Bro...just come now," Cace said right before hanging the phone up. I could tell something was wrong, but I didn't know what it was. I tried to ease my way out of the bed without waking Kreesha up, but the shit didn't work.

"Where you goin'?"

"I just got an emergency call."

"*Aww...I thought I was going to cook you breakfast and we were going to have some morning sex.*"

"*I'll take a raincheck.*" I leaned down to kiss her lips. After showering, I threw my clothes back on and headed to the warehouse.

Twenty minutes later, I was pulling up, and everyone was standing out front with sad faces. I looked around the crowd until I noticed Cace and Pete. I rushed over to them to find out what the fuck was going on.

"Yo, bro, what's good with you? What happened, why all the long faces?" I asked, curious.

"He's gone, man," Cace said just above a whisper.

"What, my nigga, who gone? Speak the fuck up!" I snapped.

"Big Russ...he was gunned down last night leaving here. Old Man Clay found him this morning when he came to clean the parking lot. He said Russ was lying on the ground next to the car with the door wide open. They let two shots off to the back of his head, bro. Shit's crazy," Cace spoke in a sad tone.

My blood started to boil instantly. All I felt was rage coming on. I looked around and saw everyone standing around looking crazy.

"You mean to tell me somebody offed him and just left him lying here for us to find?" I barked.

"Yes, youngin'...shits sad," Pete said.

"Well, why the fuck are we here? Why are we not out looking for who the fuck did this? He helped so many of you mutha fuckas over the years. Tell me why we not paintin' the fucking city red right now?" I raged.

"Chill out, T...that's not the way we need to go about this. This is no way for the king of the empire to act," Pete said.

"First and foremost, don't tell me how the fuck to act. Russ was a father to me, and king of the empire or not, I'm going to figure out who did this shit. Cace, has anyone told the family yet?" I asked, not even paying Pete any mind. I couldn't stand his ass. He was one of the older workers, and he had been around since Russ started in the game, so I knew he was going to be a pain in my ass.

"Yes...Pete went by the house to tell them. He said they were good, but his real daughter took it the hardest. You know, she just lost her mother not even a year ago."

"Damn...I feel bad for lil' mama. Can you get with Constance and let her know that everything will be taken care of? I just need her to handle all of the arrangements, and I'll foot the bill. Get all these mutha fuckas from round here. Give me a couple of days to process this all, then I'll call a meeting." After everyone cleared out, I hopped in my ride and peeled off. It was a sad day in the city, and I had no idea how I was going to deal with this. See, to many, Russ was the man in the streets, but for me, he was much more. He was more than my boss, he was my mentor and my father. The man who taught me everything I knew.

CHAPTER 3

Rose

The parking lot at St. John's Baptist was filled to the capacity. All I did was stare out the window at all the cars that were parked. Russel 'Big Russ' Sanchez was the man in the city, and it was going to be hard for us to get passed this. Not to mention, I still wasn't over the death of my mama. What were the odds having to bury both my parents in the same year?

"You ready, little Rose?" Pete asked when he opened the door to the limo.

"Not really, but I have to do this," I said in a sad tone. Once I stepped out of the limo, Pete grabbed my hand to escort me in. The closer I got to the door, I started to feel weak, and Pete had to hold me up. When we made it into the church the first thing, I saw was my daddy's gold casket. I snatched away from Pete, ran over to the casket, and peered inside at the first man that I would ever love. I then touched his face then leaned in to kiss his cheek.

"Come on, Daddy, I need you to get up. You were supposed to fly with me to college this week." I began to pull on his arm like he was going to get up and come with me. Pete ran over to me, pulling me, trying to get me to come sit down.

"He's gone, little Rose...He's gone, baby girl." Pete tried to convince me, but I wasn't buying it.

"No, he's not, he's just resting! Now leave me alone!" I screamed. Pete said he was gone once more, and I just lost it. I was punching, kicking, and biting Pete.

"My daddy is not gone, Pete...he just can't be gone. He wouldn't leave me like this, he knows I just lost my mama. Now what am I supposed to do? What am I supposed to do?" I cried out in defeat. Pete managed to get me over to the front pew and sat me next to Constance. It was something about her that was off. I mean, her and my daddy were together for years, and I have yet to see her cry. I mean, she's shed a couple of fake tears, but if she loved him the way she said, why wasn't she losing it? Even Eboni and Essence were crying their eyes out.

"You need to calm down, Rose. Your daddy would not want you in here acting like this," Constance said, causing me to roll my eyes at her. She was right though; my daddy wouldn't want me to be acting out like this. He was the one that kept me sane at my mama's funeral, but why wasn't she crying and acting out?

"Are you hurt by this, or did you want this to happen?" I snapped, not caring what I said.

"Rose, you better watch your mouth when talkin' to me. This is not the time nor place for you to be acting like an animal," Constance said while placing her shades back on her face. I didn't even know why she had them on; she wasn't even fucking crying. I couldn't stop crying, but I was able to keep calm enough to stay seated. I sat in the front row and stared in a daze at the casket. Before I knew it, my emotions got the best of me again. The scream that left my mouth was indescribable as I poured out all the pain that was in my heart.

"Daddy, why would you do this to me? You knew I needed you," I cried out. I felt a pair of arms wrap around me.

"Shhh...Rose, everything is going to be ok, boo," Honor said while she rocked me. I didn't know where she came from, but I knew I needed someone at this very moment. Honor and I had been texting ever since the night I almost got raped. She would shoot me some encouraging text messages daily since I hadn't come outside.

It was the end of the service, and everyone was making their way up to see my daddy one last time. I wasn't sure if I wanted to go up there or not, but Honor encouraged me to. She grabbed my hand and walked me up there. I walked up to the casket and stared at him then leaned in to kiss his cheek once more.

"Daddy, I will forever miss you," I said right before I turned to walk away.

"Do you wanna ride with me to the burial?" Honor asked. I didn't say anything, but I did nod my head up and down letting her know I was cool with that. Once we made it to the burial, I just stood to the back. This was the worst part of the funeral, and I just couldn't be up there with everyone else.

"You good, little Rose?" Pete asked.

"No Pete, and I'll never be ok. Do you know who did this?" I asked, shocking the hell out of myself.

"No, baby girl, I don't have no idea, but Thorne is looking into it." I heard that name plenty of times, but I'd never seen him. My daddy kept anything that had to do with work far from the house. The only one that knew what the inside of our home looked like was Pete. He had been my dad's friend for some time now.

"I don't wanna go to the repast, Pete. I wanna be dropped off at home. I had enough of this day."

"I'll make sure you get there, baby girl. Don't even worry about that."

After the burial, Pete drove me home in his car, and Constance and her girls took the limo to the repast. They had rented out a ballroom for the repast, and I knew I wasn't feeling up to being around all those people. Once we pulled up to the house, I jumped out of the car, and Pete stopped me.

"You sure you gon' be ok here alone? I know it's rough, baby girl, but we all gon' get through this. Your daddy and I were more like brothers, and I'm going to make sure his family is good no matter what."

I gave Pete a little smile and made my way into the house. Once I locked the house up, I made my way to the shower. I couldn't wait to wash this day away.

****

I had been in my room for two days. I hadn't gotten out of the bed to even wash my ass. I was still in my feelings and wasn't sure if I would ever be able to get over this. The sound of my curtains being snatched open causing the sun to shine right in my face caused me to get angry.

"Girl, it's time for you to get your fat ass up. You haven't even gotten washed since the funeral. This is unacceptable, Rose. Get the hell up now!" Constance yelled.

"Please leave me alone. I'm not bothering you, and besides, I'm in my own room stinking it up. How did you get in here anyway?" I sassed, wanting her to leave me the hell alone.

"Rose, this is my house. I could get in any room I want to get into. Now get the fuck up!" Constance yelled. I didn't pay her any mind though; I just continued to lay there. She didn't say anything else, she just walked out of the room. I rolled back over and pulled the covers back over my head. The feeling of hot water being thrown on me caused me to jump up instantly.

"What the fuck!" I yelled while jumping up and wiping the water out of my eyes. It was hot as fuck but not enough to burn my body.

"I bet you next time you'll listen. Now clean this shit the fuck up and come downstairs."

Sudden rage came over me, and I charged at Constance causing her to hit the floor. I got on top of her and started smacking her.

"Aargh...I told you to leave me alone."

"You little bitch...get your fat ass off me!" Constance yelled while trying to push me off of her.

"All you had to do was leave me alone, but no, you wanna be a bitch today."

"You know what your problem is? You're weak. All your daddy did was baby your fat ass. Well, he ain't the fuck here no more, so you better get a handle on life, little girl. Eboni and Essence come get this fat bitch off me!" she yelled. Both her stuck up ass girls came running in my room. Once they pulled me off of her, she got up and slapped the shit out of me. I tried to get loose, but they continued to hold me.

"Y'all better not let her the fuck go either." Constance grimaced right before she kicked me in my stomach causing me to fall to the floor.

"Ouch... ouch...why the fuck you hittin' me like that?" I asked while lying on the floor balled up in a knot.

"You should have thought about that before ya fat ass hit me. Get the fuck down there and hold her!" she snapped at her girls, right before she sent a couple of kicks to my side and back. After she got done punching and kicking me, they headed out of my room.

"Clean this shit the fuck up now! I bet next time you'll think about it before you put your fat ass paws on me." As much as I wanted to say something, I just couldn't. That's how much pain I was in lying on the floor. I knew right then and there that I needed to get the fuck out of here. I just needed to find my account information. My daddy held on to it because I told him I wouldn't need it until I went off to school. I would try to find it one day this week. I knew it wouldn't be today or tomorrow due to how much pain I was in.

CHAPTER 4

Constance

Rose thought I was playing with her ass, but I wasn't. Russ wasn't here to save her little ass anymore, and it was time she learned how to do shit around here.

"Mama...why would you do that to Rose?" my oldest daughter, Essence, asked.

"Essence Marie Boyd, don't you ever ask me why I do what I do. Do you wanna be locked in the room with Rose?" I asked in a sarcastic tone.

"No Mama, I thought those locks that you put on our door was just to throw Rose off?" she asked while looking at me all crazy.

"They are, but if you wanna worry about Rose, I could give you the same treatment. I was sick of Rose and her simple ass, but I knew I had to keep her around. See, I knew Russ left her everything. Yeah, he left me something too, but his little Rose got it all. I wasn't sure exactly how much since we hadn't sat and talked to the lawyer yet, but I knew how Russ was. He didn't love me, he just put on a front. Russ never loved anyone but Rose's mother, Lela Jones. The only reason they weren't together was because of the life Russ chose to live. Russ cheated every chance he got with his precious Lela, at first, he didn't but all the sudden it was happening. When Lela kicked the bucket, it was the happiest day of my life. The only thing I didn't like about that day was knowing that Rose's fat ass had to come live with us.

"Mama...Thorne is here to see you," Eboni said while entering the foyer.

"Alright, let him in," I ordered. Thorne was the most handsome young boy out of all the men Russ had working for him. I hated how close they were, but Russ was adamant about Thorne being good people. See, I didn't trust people versus Russ trusted too many.

"Hello, Ms. Constance...How are you today?" Thorne asked when he entered.

"Well, hello, young man, what do I owe the pleasure of this visit?"

"I just wanted to come by to see how you all were holding up."

"We all are good. How are things going with you being the big man in charge now?"

"I haven't really did anything different. I handled mostly everything the same as I do now. Russ made sure of that while he was living. Are all of the girls OK?"

"Well, you just saw Eboni when she answered the door, so you know she's good. Essence just went to her room, and Rose is sleeping."

"Alright cool...I'll be stopping by every now and then to check up on y'all. One of Russ' orders was to make sure his girls were good if he wasn't around. So, you hit my line if you need anything, Ms. Constance."

The sound of banging caused me to look towards the steps. I knew it was Rose's fat ass, and she must have realized she was locked in the room.

"Eboni, go tell your sister to keep it down," I said with a raised brow. Eboni didn't ask any questions; she just did what I said.

"Is everything ok? Do y'all need me to help with something?"

"No, we are OK...as a matter of fact, come on and let me walk you out. That was nice of you to stop by to make sure we were good."

"It was no problem at all. Russ was a dad to me, and I would do anything he asked me. So, I'll come around more often to check on y'all."

"Alright, that'll be fine, but I'm assuring you that we're good," I said, heading to the door with Thorne walking behind me.

"I understand that you're fine, but I still want you to know that I'll be here when and if you or the girls ever need anything. If you can't reach me, Pete can," Thorne said while heading out the door. Once the door was closed, I ran up the steps straight to Rose's room. I pulled the key out of my pocket and opened the pad lock that I had put on the door while she was sleeping.

"What the fuck are you banging for?" I yelled as I snatched the door open.

"Constance, why do you have me locked in here?"

"I didn't wanna take any chances of you running out of here after our little disagreement. You are now one of my girls, and I wouldn't want you leaving out of here and risk something happening to you. We still don't know who killed your father, and I plan on keeping you all safe," I lied because I didn't wanna get her spooked. I even put locks on my girls' doors as well, so Rose wouldn't think I was just picking on her.

"That's some weird shit, Constance, but whatever. I'm hungry," Rose said while squeezing her fat ass around me. I didn't say shit, I just let her go. I didn't know how I was going to keep her ass here, but I was going to try.

Dinner was finished, and we all were sitting at the table eating. It was quiet, but I knew sooner or later one of them would break the silence.

"Constance, I need the key to my father's office," Rose said, breaking me from my thoughts.

"What do you need the key for his office for?" I asked.

"Well, you know I'ma about to leave for school, and I need the bank information."

"What bank information?"

"My bank information that he was holding for me until I was ready to leave for school."

"Well, the school called earlier while you were sleep, and I told them that you wouldn't be attending this semester. I figured that since you're going through a hard time right now, it would be best for you to sit this first semester out. It wouldn't be smart to try to go when you don't have a clear mind. Then you end up flunking," I lied. I hadn't talk to the school, but I made myself a mental note to contact them tomorrow.

"You may be right, but that should have been a decision you let me make on my own!" Rose sassed.

"Look Rose, I did what I did because I felt like you wouldn't have agreed with me. I feel like you always go against things I say, so I made this decision for you. Now in a couple of months if I see a change in your behavior and I feel like you're OK to go, then I'll make it happen. As far as the bank information your daddy was holding for you, he must have put it with his own, and now we have to wait for the lawyer to come over to discuss his assets." Rose looked at me like she didn't believe me, but I said it very convincing.

"So, when will the lawyer come?" Rose asked.

"In the next couple of days, he will be here."

"Alright, please keep me posted."

"I will, as a matter of fact, you ladies have to be here too," I said, letting my daughters know. Russ may not have been their daddy, but he made sure they were

good.

CHAPTER 5

Honor

"I have to hurry up and get out of here before he comes."

"Man, I don't know why you just don't wanna tell him. It's been a minute now, baby, and I'm tired of sneaking around. You younger than me, but we grown as hell."

"Cace...I'm only eighteen, and you know how Thorne is. He not gon' be feelin' this shit."

"I'm five years older than you, that's not too old. Hell, my daddy seven years older than my mama. Besides, I can take care of you, and I ain't like none of these knuckle head niggas out here; I truly only wanna be with you."

"Aww... baby, I feel the same way about you. I'm just not ready to go down this road with Thorne just yet. I promise you we can tell him soon, but just not today. Now give me a kiss and text me later on," I said while pulling Cace close to me.

Cace was Thorne's best friend, right hand, and bro for life. The last thing I wanted was their friendship to be jeopardized because a one-night stand ended up being a five-month relationship.

"Alright, and make sure ya sexy ass text me when you make it in the house safe."

"Now you know I'm not going to forget to text you."

"Oh...here, don't forget the money to get your birth control refilled, and here is some extra money to get another box of condoms."

"Shit, I'm glad you reminded me, I almost forgot to get them damn pills refilled. Thank you, baby."

"You're welcome, now get out of here, he should be pulling up any minute," Cace said while smacking me on my ass."

"Mmm...hmm... look at that thing getting bigger."

"Boy, bye...this thing been big," I said while bending over and twerking a little before I headed out of the door.

I was young, but I really felt some type of way when it came to Cace. I knew he was older, but I was no baby, and I knew how to handle a man like him. I jumped in my 2019 black Benz GLC Class that Thorne helped me purchase. Even though I didn't put much money to it, he still wanted me to come up off something. He's always taught me no matter what a nigga could do for me, I needed to be able to do for myself. That was something him and his mama made sure to teach me. I had been living with them since birth. My mama had died giving birth to me, and her one and only sister had taken me in. I would always be grateful for my Auntie Tina because I could have ended up a little lost girl in the system.

I was now pulling up to the Walgreens that was located on 46th and Westfield. All in my phone not paying attention, I ran right into someone.

"Damn...you need to watch where you're going." I looked up and saw Eboni and her sister, Essence. I remembered them both from school. Eboni was a year ahead of me, and Essence was a couple of years ahead of us both. I had been wanting to run into these bitches ever since the shit went down with Rose at the party.

"I would have said excuse me, but since you wanna be smart, I won't."

"Come on, Eboni, please don't start no shit," Essence said always being the peace maker.

"You always whining like a little bitch, Essence, and Honor, you lucky you're beneath me."

"Bitch please, beneath you how?" I laughed loud as hell. I couldn't believe this hoe.

"Everything you and your family got, you got from my step daddy."

"Well, guess what? Ya step daddy left it all to my cousin. Now leave me the fuck alone before I beat ya ass. I'm already two minutes off beating you both the fuck up for what you did to Rose." Eboni sucked her teeth while Essence looked at me with wide eyes. I didn't know what triggered her off, but I could tell something was wrong.

"We didn't do anything to Rose," Essence said in a scared tone.

"Essence, come on. I had enough of talking to this bitch," Eboni said while grabbing Essence's hand and running off to their car. Something was off by the way they were acting, but I was sure going to call or text Rose as soon as I got home. It had been a couple of days since I talked to her. I walked into the Walgreens and headed straight to the pharmacy in the back. I gave the man my prescription then sat down to wait. My phone vibrating in my pocketbook alerted me that someone was calling. I pulled the phone out, and Thorne's name was flashing across the screen. I swallowed a lump in my throat not knowing what he wanted.

"Hey, big head, what's up?" I answered.

"Hey, where you located, baby girl?"

"At the Walgreens out Pennsauken. Why, what's wrong?"

"I wanna holla at you. Meet me at the crib when you finished."

"OK," was all I said before I hung the phone up. I couldn't help but to wonder what he wanted to talk to me for.

****

"Today must be a special day. I have both my kids in the house sitting at the dinner table," My auntie Tina said with a big smile on her face.

"I'm sorry, Mama, I was so caught up in work I haven't had time, but now since I'm the boss, I should be able to be home for dinner more often." Thorne assured her.

"I sure hope so because life is short, and you can be here one day and gone the same day. I know I never agreed with your way of living, but you have helped me so much along the way, and I love you even more for that, but son, I need to start seeing you more. I'm getting older, you know. I want you to settle down and give me some damn grand kids.

"Wooh...Mama, I ain't ready for no kids. Plus, I would have to have a girl for that to happen." Thorne chuckled.

"Auntie, you too funny." I laughed while shaking my head.

"I'm serious, and Thorne knows that, but enough about that. I wanna tell you how proud of you I am. You've done so good this year, and I'm happy you graduated top of your class. At first, you were going through a rough patch, but you made it happen. You ready for cosmetology school?"

"Yes... I am. I go speak to the admissions tomorrow. I can't wait to finish, I plan on owning my own salon one day."

"Yesss...baby, speak that shit into existence."

"I am, Auntie...I am...and I wanna think you for raising me into the woman that I am today. I really appreciate you."

"Aww, baby, no thanks needed. I would have did this for any of my flesh and blood."

"I'm proud of you too, biscuit head."

"Shut up, punk!" I sassed, causing Thorne and my aunt to laugh.

"Oh yeah, baby girl...Cace told me what happened to Russ' daughter the night of the party. Why didn't you tell me about it? I didn't even know you knew her."

"I didn't think I needed to tell you because Cace handled it, and I didn't know her. I just used to see her in class, but she never really talks to anyone. Me and her have been bussin' it up since that night. I even lent her my shoulder to cry on at the funeral. I feel so bad for her; she lost both her parents in the same year. That got to be a special kind of hurt."

"Oh my...that's so sad. I hope she is able to move on from this," my auntie said in a sad tone.

"I stopped by there yesterday, and Constance said they were fine, but I didn't see Russ' daughter."

"Her name is Rose, and she doesn't bang with them all like that, so she probably was in her room. I don't trust them bougie bitches. They don't care for her, so they treat her like shit. I make it my business though to send her some uplifting text messages every day."

"That's good, keep that up for me, and I'm going to have Pete check on her as well. I need to get to know her and keep a close watch on her. I don't know who did this shit to Russ, so I need to make sure I pay close attention to his family."

"My plans are to get her to come out of the house sometimes. I'm trying to explain to her that staying cooped up in the house in her room is not healthy."

"Well, that's a good thing, baby, and make sure you keep it up. Depression is no joke, and I would hate to see her suffer from that. Son, you make sure you do as big Russ said and make sure his family is good at all times. Russ was a good man, and he made sure you grew to be the man that you are today, and I thank him for that," my auntie said.

At first, I was scared of what Thorne wanted especially since he called me right after I left Cace's house. When he questioned me about Rose, I wasn't shocked. Russ was like a daddy to him, and if Russ asked him to do anything for his family, I knew Thorne was going to provide for them no matter what.

CHAPTER 6

Thorne

Things had been running smooth with the empire. It was just a couple of things I was questioning, but I needed to keep an eye on it before I spoke on it.

"What's up, bro? What you in here doin'?" Cace asked while walking into my office.

"Nothing, just chilling. After the meeting today, I managed to put a lot in prospective."

"I already put some men on Telly's ass. For some reason, I just don't trust that nigga," Cace blurted out.

"I feel you, but check this, I've been getting some bad vibes about Pete and Dom. I'm trying to give the homie's the benefit of the doubt, but I may have to do what Russ told me to do."

"What did Russ tell you to do?" Cace asked.

"He told me to fire all the ones that I thought was going to be jealous of me taking over and give them a healthy severance. I feel like that needs to be done because if I find out these niggas doin' some foul shit, I'm going to kill them, and I'm so fucking serious."

"If you feel like you need to do what he said, go for it, but be prepared to have some beef."

"You know me, I don't give a fuck about any of that. I'll off a mutha fucka in a minute."

"Well, how about we watch them nigga's every move for a little bit and then decide what you wanna do. I don't want you just jumping into shit."

"Alright, that sounds like a plan."

Ok...good, because I need to get out of here. I have a hot date."

"When am I going to meet this chick you've been ducking off with?"

"As soon as we make this shit official, I'ma introduce y'all. Just give me time, bro, and I got you. I swear shawty got me on cloud nine."

"Wow...I never thought I would be hearing you talk like that. You serious about ol' girl I see."

"I really am, bro, the shit is crazy, because I never ever been an ol' sucka in love type nigga, but this one got me definitely in my feelings. I can't wait to take this shit to the next level."

"I'm happy as hell for you, I just hope this is really what you want. You only twenty-three, bro. We still young as fuck. You sure you ready to settle down?"

"Yup...I'm sure no matter how old you are, you know when you ready to stop playing out here in these streets. Plus, my daddy always tells me I'll know when I found the one, and I believe I found the one. You should try settling down one day. I'm sure Ms. Tina want some grands."

"Here you go with the shits. She said the same thing at dinner the other night."

"What did you tell her?"

"I told her I'm not ready yet and that I would need a girl first. I haven't met the right one yet. Plus, this street shit ain't for people who have babies. You never know when someone gon' wanna use ya family against you."

"I get it, bro, but you can't let that stop you from having kids one day. You just have to make sure you protect them with ya life. Truth be told, you could be here one minute and gone the next. No matter what you do in life, bro."

"You right...you right...but let's talk about that at a different time. Get out of here before ya girl get mad when you late and break that shit off already."

"OK...I'm out. Hit my line when you leave here. You know I don't like leaving you here alone because of what happened to Russ here."

"I'm good...security still here. They have new hours, no one is never to be left in here alone ever. So, if we got business going on, then they have to stay longer."

Everyone had been on edge since the shit happened to Russ but me. The reason why was because I thought I had a feeling who was behind this shit. I was trying to get everything sorted out before I brought it to the light, but then I thought, *it is what it is.* Then this was the reason why Russ was acting kind of funny towards the end of his life. The crazy part of all of this was I just didn't understand why they would do this to him. I guess I was more so in shock about this all. I hoped my theory wasn't true.

"Bro...I'm out. You don't hear me?" Cace yelled bringing me out of my thoughts.

"My fault, I had some shit on my mind, but go ahead, get out of here. I'll be OK." I assured Cace, and he walked out the door. My phone started going off, and I looked down and saw it was Kree. I wasn't beat for her tonight, so I just hit the ignore button. My ass was kind of hungry, so I decided to get up and head to The Cheesecake Factory to have me a late dinner before I headed home. After locking up my office and bussin' it up with the security team for a hot second, I made my way out of the door. I jumped in my truck and peeled off.

Breaking every traffic violation, you could name, I was now pulling up in front of the restaurant in ten minutes flat. On my way in the restaurant, my phone started to go off again, and it was Kree. I didn't know what was going on with her ass, but I just wasn't in the mood to deal with anyone. I just wanted to eat and take my black ass home.

"Hello, welcome to The Cheesecake Factory. I'm Lauren, will you be dining alone?" I looked up from my phone, and this cute, light-skinned chick was smiling in my face. I looked at her and smiled back before I spoke.

"Yes...beautiful, I'll be dining alone."

"Alright, well let me show you to your table," she said while handing the dude who I assumed was the one that was supposed to show me to my seat the menus. I couldn't do shit but laugh while shaking my head. Baby girl was walking in front of me swaying them hips from side to side hard as fuck. Little mama had a body to die for, and she was pretty as fuck. I knew I didn't do this often, but I wanted her number. Once we made it to the table, I pulled the chair out and sat down then stared at her for a second, taking in her beauty once more.

"Thank you, Ms. Lauren...Now can you do me a favor and put your number in my phone?" I asked while sliding my phone across the table. She hurried and grabbed it up and began to program her number in.

"Here you go, Mr.—" she said, throwing me a hint that I hadn't given her my name just yet.

"My name is Thorne, ma," I said while licking my lips.

"Thorne, hmm...that's different but cute. What would you like to drink, Mr. Thorne?"

"I would like a raspberry lemonade to come out with my meal and a Heineken right now while I wait."

"Ok, no problem, would you like an appetizer to go with your beer?"

"Nah..." I said while picking the menu up.

"Alright...well it was nice meeting you, Thorne. Your waiter will be right over."

"OK ma, and I'll be calling your sexy ass real soon," I said while shooting her a wink. Baby girl left my table all smiles. I usually didn't do shit like this. Hell, chicks would flock to me every time they saw me, but shit, I was single and her little ass was fine, short, and thick as fuck.

I was all into the menu trying to figure out what I wanted when a familiar voice called my name. I looked up, and it was Constance, Eboni, and Essence.

"Well, hello ladies. How's everyone feeling this evening?" I asked.

"We are fine, young man. I told you the last time you saw us, and I told Pete to let you know we were fine," Constance said. It was like the girls didn't speak unless she gave them permission. I knew it was Eboni that spoke to me because I knew her little hoe ass had a crush on me, but I wouldn't give her the time of day. Those chicks got around, the shit was crazy as fuck. I looked at everyone and noticed I didn't see Rose. This was my second time seeing them and not seeing Rose.

"That's good to hear, Ms. Constance, but why the girls never talk when they around you? I know they can because when they not around you, they runnin' them mouths like crazy, especially Eboni. She been tryna get on this dick forever." I chuckled. The look Constance gave me was funny as fuck. I was tired of acting like I liked her strong-face having ass. I didn't even know how I was going to keep that shit going. I mean, I would still check on them and get Pete to do the same, but enough was enough. I didn't like how she had her girls trained; the shit was crazy, and it explained why when they weren't around her, they acted like a couple of bitches in heat.

"Young man, I will not tolerate disrespect."

"I wasn't being disrespectful; I was being real. Where's Rose at?" I asked, really wanting to know the truth.

"Rose is home sleeping like always. She's really been going through it since she's lost both of her parents."

"That's funny to me, Constance, and you wanna know why?" I asked while running my fingers through my beard.

"What do you mean, Thorne?"

"I've been asking you every time I see you, and I've sent Pete to check on y'all too. Every single time the response is everybody is doing good, but here it is right now, you're telling me Rose is having a hard time dealing with this, which is to be expected, but why have y'all been lying to me telling me that everyone is good? The one thing I can't stand is a fucking liar. So once again, where is Rose at?"

"I told you she's home sleeping and let me explain something to you; you may have been left to run Russell's empire, but you don't run shit over here, little boy. We are doing fine, and we will continue to do fine. So, therefore, you don't have to keep coming to check on us. Come on, let's go, daughters!" Constance snapped, and Eboni and Essence ran right behind her. Something about this old, ugly Naomi Campbell-looking bitch wasn't right, and I was going to find out what she was up to.

CHAPTER 7

Rose

A week had gone by since I had asked Constance for my paperwork out of my daddy's office and her stupid ass still hadn't given me anything. I was sure the school would have been calling me by now, but I hadn't received any voicemails or missed calls. I peeled my tired body out of bed and made my way into the bathroom. For some reason, I had been finding myself sleep all the time. I really didn't think anything of it. I just figured my body was just drained from all the crying and sadness. I checked my door before heading into the bathroom, and of course, it was locked. Constance thought I was a dummy; I knew damn well she didn't keep us all locked in the room because the house was always quiet, so I knew her and her stupid ass daughters were out and about. I didn't care because I didn't wanna go out anyway. I was still in my feelings about my parents, and truth be told, I didn't know when or if I would ever get over it. I walked in the bathroom and looked in the mirror and wanted to cry. My hair was all over the place. I had bags under my eyes, and they were red and puffy. I didn't know where the bags came from considering all the sleep I had been getting. I was sure depression had set in because I felt like I was back in the same dark space I was in when I lost my mama. This time, it felt ten times worse. My daddy and I had gotten a lot closer since I had moved in, and some stupid mutha fuckas took him from me. A lonely tear started to fall down my cheek, and I really didn't wanna do this today. I wiped my face before any more tears started to fall then placed my wild hair in a ponytail so I could hop in the shower.

After my shower, I felt clean and relaxed but still numb. All I wanted to do was crawl back up into the bed and cry my heart out. A knock at my room door brought me out of my thoughts.

"What the fuck y'all knockin; for? I can't even open the fucking door!" I yelled knowing it was Constance and her dumb ass daughters. After I yelled, I heard the locks being removed, and Constance and her ugly duckling daughters walked in.

"That is not the way you talk to the person that is bringing you food," Constance sneered.

"First of all, I didn't ask for anything to eat, so you can take that shit right back with you. Secondly, who said I wanted to eat up here? I wanna eat downstairs at the kitchen table just like you and ya girls!" I snapped while squeezing by them and making my way out of the door.

"Listen, little girl, I'm so sick of you and that smart ass mouth. If you wanna eat then you will eat this. If not, then you don't fucking eat at all," Constance fussed while following behind me with her little trolls behind her."

"Well, I guess I won't eat then. I'll just grab me a water."

"Yeah, ya fat ass could stand to miss a couple of meals."

"You stay with the fat jokes, but it's cool. If I wanna lose weight I could, but you and ya ugly ass daughters can't change those faces without some type of surgery.

All y'all walking around with faces only a mother could love." I giggled while making my way into the living room to sit on the couch. Once I sat down, I could feel them all staring at me all crazy. I didn't care though; I wasn't in the mood to be dealing with them.

"Constance, when are you going to let me in my daddy's office to get my banking information?" I asked.

"I looked in there already, and I didn't see it. Maybe he put it in a different place. I'll reach out to Mr. Shults later on. He contacted me the other day and told me there was no need to read the will. Russ had left all his assets to me. Whatever he left to you he made it so that you don't get it until you finish college. Mr. Shults has your paperwork. When he came over, you were sleeping, and Eboni couldn't wake you up."

For some reason, I wasn't buying none of the shit she had just said to me. I had to find out this lawyer's info so I could talk to him on my own. The only way I would be able to do that was if I talked to Pete. I made a mental note to shoot Pete a text when I got back up to my room. I knew I could count on him to get the information I needed. I grabbed the TV remote and turned it on. I felt like sitting downstairs for a little while since I was always in my room.

A couple of hours went by, and Eboni and Essence had gone to bed, and Constance was still sitting in the living room watching me like a hawk. Her ass was strange; I just couldn't put my finger on it. Not wanting to be in her presence anymore. I made my way up to my room. Once I made it inside, I closed the door and grabbed my phone. I saw I had a missed call, and it was from Honor. It was odd because she never really called me, she usually just text me daily to make sure I was good. I was feeling like I could maybe use a friend since I knew I was going through a depressive state. I decided to go ahead and give her a call back. I dialed her number, and she picked up on the second ring.

"Hey, you...what's been going on?"

"Hey...I'm OK, just trying to make it. How have you been? I was shocked to see a missed call from you."

"Yeah...I figured I'm always texting, let me call and see how you doin'."

"That's nice of you. I want you to know I really appreciate you. From day one, you've been nothing but good to me, and I'll forever be grateful."

"No problem, ma...I saw you needed help, and I didn't mind helping. I know you're going through a rough time, but I wanted to get you out of that house. Do you think you would wanna go out with me Friday?"

"I don't know. I just be in my room and sleeping all the time. Maybe we can wait till Friday gets here and see how I'm doing then."

"Alright, that's fine, we can just play it by ear."

"Yeah, let's just do it that way because some days are worse than others. Sometimes, I can get up, then others, I'm just out of it."

"Have you went to the doctor? If not, maybe you should, babes."

"No...because I know it's just depression setting in, and I'll push through to get myself together as soon as I stop grieving."

"It was just a suggestion, but listen, I have to go. I'll be checking up on you through text message as usual. You take care of yourself, and I'll call you Friday."

"Ok...and I'll try," I said, right before I hung my phone up. Once I hung the phone up, I laid across the bed staring at the ceiling until I drifted off to sleep.

CHAPTER 8

Constance

Rose had me so angry, I didn't know what to do. I bet I'd think next time before I left them simple ass daughters of mine in the house alone. I couldn't believe they let her fucking leave the house. I left specific orders for they dumb asses to lock her in the room before they went to bed.

"What's wrong with you? We haven't been together in so long, and you sittin' here in another world. What, you don't miss me?" Pete asked, bringing me out of my thoughts.

"Nothing, baby...I'm sorry my attention is on other things. The girls have been driving me crazy. All I wanna do is relax, but it seems like it's always something going on with them," I lied, trying to channel my anger. I was so pissed off they didn't keep an eye on Rose. It was two of them, and they both couldn't do shit right.

"They goin' through some shit right now, Connie, just cut them some slack," Pete said, calling me by my nickname he would call me whenever we were alone.

"I'm trying, baby, but you don't know how hard it's been hard trying to keep them all on a straight path including Rose. She has been a bit much lately, and I'm not sure I can take her much longer."

"I told you to let her go ahead to school, but no, you want to hold her here as a hostage. You already knew how Russ felt about her and Thorne, so you knew he was going to make sure the two of them were forever good. You can't be sitting around here being bitter because of him not leaving you much. You already had your own money when you got with him, so I know you good."

Pete was right, but to know that you've been married to a man for so many years and he just leaves you nothing but the house and a couple of cars, the shit bothered me like crazy. I kind of figured Russ didn't love me, but this stunt right here showed me everything. The day we met up with the lawyer played in my head over and over again.

"Hello everyone...I'm sorry we had to meet under these circumstances, but this won't take long at all. Where's Ms. Rose Sanchez?" Mr. Shultz, our family lawyer, asked.

"She couldn't make it today, and I didn't wanna keep prolonging the meeting."

"Ok...well she will need to come see me so I can tell her everything she needs to know."

"You can just tell me what you need to tell her, and I'll be sure to give her the message."

"I'm sorry, Mrs. Sanchez. I can only tell her this. Russel gave strict request in his will. Now let's get this started."

"Yes...please because I have shit to do, and being here wasn't one of them," Thorne said causing me to roll my eyes. I swear I was growing tired of this young man. Pete tried to convince me that he was just concerned, but I wasn't buying that shit. His little ass was up to something. I just wasn't sure exactly what it was.

"Well, Mr. Williams, it won't take long at all, and I would like everyone to stay until I'm finished. Mrs. Sanchez, I'll start with you. Russel has left you the house and all of the cars except for the midnight blue Camaro. He left that one to Ms. Rose. Alright Mr. Williams, you're up next."

"Wait a minute, out of all the shit Russ had, I was only left with the house and cars?" I snapped.

"I'm afraid so, ma'am. Now, Mr. Williams, of course you know you've been left with the Sanchez empire. Plus, the main bank account. Mr. Sanchez also wanted you to have the new bar and grill that was set to open in four months. He said everything is already a go, you just have to proceed with the grand opening, and he trusts you to do it and go out with a bang."

"This has got to be a mistake. Russ would have never did things this way. I don't believe this at all!" I yelled out causing everyone who was in the room to look at me.

"I'm afraid this is what he wanted. There are more things to discuss, but it's all for Ms. Rose. He also wanted me to tell you this, Mrs. Sanchez. Whatever happens in the dark, always come to the light. I'm not gon' blast you, but know, I already know, and your karma is coming, my dear wife."

"What you over here thinking about?" Pete asked while climbing on top of me.

"I just can't believe Russ did me like this. I swear he knew about us, and that's what he meant in the letter he left Shultz."

"That may be true, but baby, he is gone, and it ain't nothin' he can do to hurt us. Now come on and show me some love. It's been a minute, and I've been missing you like crazy," Pete said while placing soft kisses on my forehead then each of my cheeks. Pete then began to trail down my body making sure to not miss a beat. He now was face to face with my love tunnel ready to dive in. Once Pete got started, he began to flick his tongue on my clit in a fast motion. I moaned out in pleasure enjoying the feeling. After a couple more flicks of his tongue, Pete had the juices running all out of me. The minute my body stopped shaking, Pete made his way back up to my lips and kissed me passionately. While he used his hand to spread my legs wide open in a V position, I rested my legs on his chest, and he slid right into my love tunnel. He began to give me long, deep strokes as he used his fingers and played with my clit while he eased in and out of me.

"Shit Pete...just like that, baby," I cooed while enjoying him hitting my spot.

"Mmm...hmm...that thing wet as hell. You really been missin' me, huh?" Pete asked while moving in and out of me in a fast motion. Pete continued to drill in and out of me just like I liked it. I could tell from his movements that he was just about to reach his peak.

"I'm about to cum, baby...how about you cum with me?" Pete asked, causing my body to react. He sped up the pace, making sure to go deeper, hitting every spot you could possibly think of.

"I'm about to cum with you, baby...shit I'm cummin' right now," I moaned out in pleasure as my body began to shake. Pete and I both came long and hard. After we both were able to get ourselves together, we just laid there in each other's embrace.

"So, what you thinkin' about now?" Pete asked.

"Do you think Thorne is going to be a problem?" I asked curious.

"A problem for what? Nobody knows about us Connie, so just relax, and if they do find out, so what?

Russ not here anymore. Shit, we can make it look like we got together while grieving, or we could just do us and not give a fuck what people think. I'm single, and you're a widow, and that's that. Now, stop worrying so much."

"I feel like if they find out about us, then it's a possibility, they'll find out about everything."

"Connie, I told you no one will find out anything, and you must not bring this up anymore. Just act like nothing ever happened, and we will be just fine." Pete assured me.

I always try to believe him, but I just wasn't sure he was right. I had a feeling everything that we had done was sure going to come back and bite us in the ass. One thing my mama always said to me growing up was karma was a real bitch.

CHAPTER 9

Honor

I was so glad Rose was able to come out tonight. I could see all in her eyes that she was going through something deep. I couldn't imagine losing both my parents at the age I was now. Shit I hurt sometimes thinking about not having a mama now, but our situations were different since I didn't even remember my mama. She died before I even got in this world good. Rose knew her parents and grew with them. That shit had to be hard to deal with.

"Honor...I know you hear me calling you," Rose said.

"My fault boo I'm over here in another world. I'm so glad you came out with me tonight. I'm surprised your wicked ol' stepsisters didn't try to come out."

"I don't fuck with them at all."

"Essence seem like she could be cool, but that damn Eboni, I don't know about her crazy ass. She is so in love with my cousin, Thorne, but he won't give her the time of day."

"Thorne, I hear that name often, but still haven't met him. I know my daddy loved him like a son."

"Yeah...him and Russ were super tight. My cousin is a good dude; he's the reason why me and my auntie are always straight."

"If you don't mind me asking, where's your parents at?"

"My mama died giving birth to me, and I never knew who my pops was."

"Oh wow...I'm sorry to hear that."

"It's cool...it doesn't bother me like it did when I was younger. Rose, you good?" I asked because she had gotten quiet and started staring off into space.

"My fault, I'm good. Ain't we supposed to be turning up?" Rose asked standing up to dance. I couldn't help but to laugh because baby girl had no rhythm.

We were at Club Vera enjoying ourselves. Yeah, we were underage, but I knew the dude at the door, and he let us right in. The music was good, and the drinks were everything. He had us in the VIP, and he had a waitress hooking us up all night.

"Girl, where did you learn to dance like that?" I giggled.

"Damn, am I that bad?" Rose asked in a sad tone.

"I mean, you not that bad, just a little stiff and off beat. Let me show you how it's done, baby."

"Rich nigga, eight figure, that's my type,
That's my type, nigga that's my type,
Eight inch big, ooh, that's good pipe,
Bad bitch, I'ma ride the dick all night..."

My Type by *Saweetie* blasted through the speakers. I jumped up so fast to show Rose how I got down. I loved to dance, so it wasn't about nothing to show her.

"Where did you learn to dance like that?" Rose asked.

"Watching videos and shit like that."

"Oh OK, well I'ma need you to show me one day."

"You know I got you. Now tell me how you've really been doing?"

"To be honest with you, Honor, I've been doing nothing but sleeping. You would think I was taking something, but I'm not. I just think depression is sitting in to be honest. I really would love to thank you for getting me out of the house. I almost didn't make it."

"Aww...well, I'm glad you decided to come out."

"Y'all ladies good?" my boy Quan asked.

"Yeah, we straight, and thanks again; me and my friend needed this night out."

"You already know it's no problem, Honor. I got you always, beautiful. Now let me go back out to this door. I'll be back over to check on y'all in a little while."

Rose and I continued to laugh, joke, and drink the whole time we were there. The night was so cool, I was shocked no drama had broken out.

"You just don't know how to stay out of my dude's face, huh, Honor?" a familiar voice said bringing me out of my thoughts.

"Well hello, Tyrah...how you been, girl?" I asked dryly.

"Bitch, don't speak to me. I just saw Quan coming from up here, and I know he the one that got ya little young ass in here. I wonder if Thorne know ya little thirsty ass in here!" Tyrah sassed.

"Honor, what's going on?" Rose asked green to the whole situation.

Nothing boo...this hoe think I want her old ass man. Let me handle this, hold my purse and my phone."

I jumped up so fast and delivered two punches straight to her face. I was sick of every time she saw me, she talked shit. Plus, she was starting to use the bitch word too freely these days like I was a punk or something. I got on top of Tyrah's punk ass and continued to beat her the fuck up. By now, it was a crowd around us in VIP, and I knew the club was about to get shut down.

"Bitch, I know you done lost ya damn mind. You better get the fuck off my cousin." The chick that was with Tyrah finally realized what the fuck was going on. She tried to sneak a hit in, but Rose had jumped up and was all in her face. Next thing I knew, the chick had hit Rose, and why did she do that? Rose had so much pinned up anger in her, she knocked that bitch the fuck out then started stomping her ass. We both were drunk as hell in a whole brawl in the VIP section of the club. I was still throwing punch after punch until I felt my body being snatched off her simple ass.

"Honor, what the fuck you doin' out here wildin', ma? Do Thorne even know you in here?" one of the dudes that worked for my cousins asked. I looked over, and another one of his goons had Rose. I couldn't believe this shit. I was trying to be sneaky, now Thorne was gon' be pissed and so would Cace.

"The bitch came up here starting with me, so I beat her ass. I don't care about Thorne feeling some type of way. I keep telling you niggas I'm grown as hell. Now put me the fuck down, Dre!" I snapped.

"No...not till we get out the door and to my car. Them boys is on the way here, and if ya little ass don't wanna go to the county, you better chill the fuck out and sober the fuck up. Where baby girl that's with you going?"

"She is coming with me, that's Rose, Big Russ' daughter." I let him know, and right then and there he knew what it was. Once we made it outside, Dre gave Pooh my keys and demanded him to follow him.

"You always on something, Honor. You know damn well you weren't old enough to be in that damn club.

Now I have to disturb Thorne because ya little ass don't know how to act."

"Nigga...I'm grown and Thorne ain't my damn daddy. Thorne boss you niggas around not me."

"I'm not gon' comment because I know that ain't shit but that liquor talking, and you, little mama, what ya stepmoms gon' say about you being in a club and you not twenty-one?"

"Fuck her and how she feels," Rose said and leaned her head back on the seat. After Rose and I both curse Dre's dumb ass out, he didn't say anything else. He just pulled his phone out and called Thorne then peeled off.

CHAPTER 10

Thorne

The phone call I had just gotten had me pissed off to the max. Honor knew I didn't play about her going into clubs knowing her little ass wasn't old enough. The only way she would be able to was if it was an event or something I was throwing. The person I was out here in these streets had me extra careful about the things I allowed her to do. She always got pissed off, but I only did this for her safety. My phone rung bringing me out of my thoughts.

"What's good with you, Dre? Y'all here yet?"

"Yeah, but her little stubborn ass won't get out of the car. Talking about she doesn't live here, and why didn't I take her home?"

"Alright, here I come." I threw on my Nike slides and a beater then made my way out the front door. When I made it to the car, Honor was sitting in the front seat with her arms crossed and lips poked out.

"Honor, if you don't get the fuck out of this car. I'ma pull ya spoiled ass out."

"Thorne, I don't wanna be here, I wanna go home to my own house."

"If you get out of the car, I'll take you home. Now come the fuck on, girl!" I snapped.

I wasn't taking her little ass nowhere tonight; she was going right to the guest room. I wasn't about to play with this brat tonight.

"Who that in the backseat?" I asked.

"Oh yeah, that's Big Russ' daughter. I was trying to tell you that before you hung up on me."

After Honor got out the front seat, she stormed her drunk ass in the house forgetting all about her little friend. I opened the car door, and baby girl was out. All I saw was her thick ass thighs peeking out of the little black skirt she had on. I tapped her on the shoulder to wake her up, she stared at me for a second then started to giggle. I couldn't do shit but shake my head. These two knew better than to be out drinking like this when they were underage. I mean, I didn't mind Honor drinking; she was about to be nineteen in a couple of months, but she needed to be in the comfort of her home if she wanted to drink not out in the streets when anything could happen to her.

"So, you're Thorne?" she asked, still giggling.

"Come on, lil' mama, let's get you in the house," I said, helping her get out of the car.

"Will I be safe in your house?" she slurred her words.

"Yes...you'll be good," I said, finally getting her to follow me.

"Alright Thorne, I'm out. I'll hit you tomorrow before I come to the spot."

"Ok, bro, and good looking."

"No problem...you already know."

Dre pulled off, and I hurried to get baby girl in the crib. When we made it inside, Honor was lying on the couch starting to doze off. I tapped her on the arm to get her attention. I needed her to make her way upstairs to one of the guest rooms. She rolled her eyes and sucked her teeth, but she got her little ass up and followed me. Since I didn't want Rose to wake up tripping in an unfamiliar place, I went ahead and let them both go in the same guest room. Once we made it into the room, no words were spoken, they both came out their shoes and laid across the bed. I covered them with a blanket and turned the lights off. All I could do was shake my head on my way to my room. I shot my mama a text letting her know that I had Honor's grown ass here with me. Then I powered my business phone off, put my personal phone on vibrate, and laid my tired ass down. I would handle Honor's ass in the morning.

******

No matter what time I went to bed, I was an early riser. I would get up and go to the gym, but this morning I got up and did a jog around my neighborhood. I walked back in my crib and heard noises coming from the kitchen. I was sure it wasn't anybody but Honor, but to my surprise, Rose was sitting at my table. I stood in the doorway and stared at her for a minute taking in her beauty. She appeared to be staring off into space. The minute I walked all the way into the kitchen, she looked up at me.

"Good morning," she said in a low tone.

"What's good, lil' mama? How you feeling this morning?"

"My head hurts a little, but I took the Tylenol I had in my purse when I got up."

"Honor still sleeping?" I asked.

"Yes...I tried waking her up because I didn't wanna just be walking all over your house. She wouldn't budge though."

"You good, ma...are you hungry?"

"Not really, my stomach doesn't feel right."

"That's all that drinking y'all were doing last night, but I'll get you some fresh fruit so you can put a little something on your stomach. While I do that, tell me how did y'all get into the place?"

"Honor was just trying to get me out of the house, since I've been going through it. Losing my parents has taken a toll on me, and living with my stepmother doesn't make the shit any better. So, please don't go hard on her. She was just trying to get me out of this depression mode I've been in."

Hearing her say that made me sad. All of a sudden, I wanted to make her feel better. I wanted to help her get through this hard time, but she still hadn't answered my question.

"I'm sorry to hear that, but you still didn't answer my question, lil' mama." I hinted.

"My fault, I just don't think you should come off on her when she was only worried about my well-being."

"Lil' mama, once again, I'm sorry for what you going through, but you have yet to answer my question, and you kind of pissing me off."

"Thorne...whatever you wanna know, just ask me. Don't be in here interrogating my damn friend!" Honor snapped while walking into the kitchen.

"Here you go waking up with that smart-ass mouth. We gon' talk about this shit, Honor, and I mean it. I don't know how many times I keep telling you not to do the same shit." I chastised, turning my attention back to what I was doing.

"Yeah...that's your problem, you keep making all these rules and regulations when I'm grown, Thorne. You can't keep the hand cuffs on me forever. Auntie Tina doesn't even hound me like you do. I graduated with good grades and will be starting cosmetology school in a month and starting an online business course in a couple of weeks. Then I plan to open my own salon. It's not many chicks out here that have made it this far with their parents not in their live. Yes, you and Auntie Tina have given me the world and raised me to be the woman I am today, but Thorne, you have to give me a break sometimes. I know you mean well, cuz, but you have to let me learn from my own mistakes.

"Whatever Honor, you may be eighteen, but you ain't twenty-one. So, you still have to go by my rules. I don't care if you like it or not."

"Thorne, you not my fuckin' daddy, and I'm out. Come on, Rose, I'll drop you off at home!" Honor sassed and walked out.

Rose got up and followed behind Honor. I couldn't help but to watch her thick ass walk out. She seemed so innocent, quiet, and green to everything. I knew Russ kept her away from what he had going on, but to actually meet her, I could tell she was a good girl. I didn't say shit else to Honor, I just let her simple ass go.

CHAPTER 11

Rose

After Honor dropped me off, when I walked into the house, it was empty. I made my way right to my daddy's office. When I got there, I noticed that Constance's ugly ass had put another lock on the door. I ran to the kitchen to find a knife to see if I could break the lock. This bitch was doing all types of extra shit. If she didn't have anything to hide, why would she put another lock on the door?

After a good forty-five minutes, I got tired of trying to break the lock, and my headache was getting worse. I just threw the knife on the floor and took my tired ass to my room. I had to find a way to get away from this crazy bitch. Me not having any money was in the fucking way.

Once I made it to my room, I stripped out of my clothes and made my way to the shower. I turned my phone to 702 Pandora station then sat my phone on the sink before I hopped in the tub.

"I don't really wanna stay,
I don't really wanna go,
But I really need to know,
Can we get it together?"

Get it together by 702 played from my phone while I let the water run over my head. I needed this shower to feel relaxed. I poured my Dove body wash on my washcloth and started to wash my body. Thoughts of my night came to mind, and I had to admit I was having a good time until the fight broke out. I was a little intoxicated, but I remember everything that happened. I even remembered Thorne helping me out of the car and giggling at him. That man was fine as hell, and he smelled so damn good. I could tell he was overprotective over Honor, and I could tell it was getting on her nerves.

I felt a swift gush of cold air against my skin. I knew the shower curtain had to be snatched open. Before I got the chance to turn to see who it was, I felt sting after sting hitting my wet skin. So busy trying to guard myself from the hits, I ended up slipping in the tub.

"You think you the fuck grown now, leaving your fat ass out of my house and not coming back. What the fuck is wrong with you, Rose? I keep telling you as long as you under my roof, you have to go by my rules. Your daddy let you get away with the most, but you got the right one now!" Constance yelled while she continued to hit my wet body with a leather belt. Hearing her mention my daddy, I felt hurt. I felt defeated, and I was at the point I didn't even wanna be on earth anymore. I didn't try to fight back, all I did was continue to shield my body.

"Mama...stop it, you're going to kill her!" I heard Essence yell.

"That bitch will be fine. Now help her get cleaned up. I bet next time she knows better than to stay out all night and not call to let me know she's ok," Constance said on her way out of the bathroom.

"Come on, Rose, let me help you," Essence said while helping me out of the tub. I didn't like her ass, but I knew she meant well. If it wasn't for her, Constance would still have been beating me with the belt.

"Why is she doing this to me?" I managed to get out through the pain.

"To be honest with you, Rose, I don't know, but you have to stop getting on her bad side. It seems like since ya daddy been gone and he didn't leave her much, she's been really tripping. Don't think she hasn't been acting different with us because she has. She just treats you worse than us because you talk back, we don't." Essence assured me.

I didn't respond, I just continued moving in slow motion. My body was sore as hell, and all I wanted to do was lay down. Hearing Essence say my daddy didn't leave Constance much piqued my interest. Constance and Russ had been together for ever; if he didn't leave her much of anything, it must have been a good reason why. I was going to look into this shit if it was the last thing I did.

****

The rain hitting my window woke me up from my deep slumber. I peeled myself out of the bed and made my way to the bathroom. I felt so damn groggy I had no clue what was wrong with me. Once I finished using the bathroom and brushing my teeth, I walked back into my room and sat on my bed. I looked on the dresser and noticed my phone was gone. I hopped up and checked the door, and to my surprise, it was open. I then made my way downstairs to see if anyone had seen my phone. When I made it downstairs, they all were sitting at the dining room table getting ready for breakfast.

"Good morning, Rose...I was just about to send your plate upstairs. You've been knocked out since after lunch yesterday." I wasn't aware of sleeping that long. I needed to get to the doctor to see why I was sleeping so much. I remember crying myself to sleep after the day she beat me in the shower which was two days ago. After Essence had stayed in the room with me and kept me company, she had gotten me something to eat and something for pain. After that, I had slept all the way till dinner the next day. So, the next time I ate after that was yesterday at lunch time. This shit was getting crazy, and maybe it was time for me to go see a doctor like Honor said.

"Have any of you seen my phone?" I asked.

"Oh, about that...the day all that went on in your bathroom, it fell into the toilet."

"OK...so when will you be getting me another one?"

"I won't be...I don't do shit for little girls that don't listen." '

"Constance, you sound dumb as fuck. I keep telling you I'm not a little girl. I'm grown as fuck!" I snapped.

"You little bitch, you ain't grown til you're able to get out on your own, and from the looks of it, your broke ass don't have anything, so you'll be here longer than what you expected. See ya daddy didn't leave your banking information; as a matter of fact, nobody knows where it is, so you don't have a dime, and I'll be damned if I give your fat ass anything. Yeah, Russ was the best daddy in the world, huh? If that was so, why did he leave all his shit to a boy that's not even his blood? He just left his one and only daughter and his loving wife here on earth without anything. Some fucking good man he was. He probably took your money and got it all in this drug shit. Thorne probably has your money too. Just like he has everything else," Constance ranted.

I snatched my plate from her and made my way back to my room with tears in my eyes. I didn't know whether to believe her or not. I just wasn't too sure. My daddy did care about the street shit more than he did me. That was one of the reasons him and my mama didn't make it. Once I made it to my room, I cried for a little then ate my food. I then laid the plate on the floor and curled up in my bed in a knot.

Daddy, what the hell was you thinking leaving me here with this lady? Why the fuck would you do this to me? I yelled out as if he was really there listening to me talk. I had to find out what really was going on. I knew good and got damn well that my daddy wouldn't have left me with anything. I needed to talk to Pete like yesterday, but the bitch took my damn phone. I guess I would have to use Essence to get what I needed since I no longer had access to a phone.

CHAPTER 12

Constance

"Connie, what the fuck you got goin' on? You goin' about this all wrong."

"Pete... last I checked, I was the one in charge of how this was going to go down."

"You right, until you started doing dumb shit. You gon' keep putting ya hands on that damn girl and end up dead or in jail."

"Her punk ass ain't doing shit. She's sleeping too much to get up and do anything," I said while twirling my fingers in my hair.

Pete was getting on my fucking nerves; this was one of the reasons why Russ wouldn't leave the empire to him. He knew Pete couldn't handle it. Pete was a bitch ass nigga, but the dick game was great. Which was why for years I continued to cheat on Russ with him. Shit, Russ did him from time to time, so what was wrong with me doing me?

"Connie, what you mean she's been sleeping? What the hell have you been doing to that damn girl?"

"Pete, would you just chill out? Everything is going to be OK. I'm not gon' kill the little bitch. I just want her to listen and sit the fuck still, that's it. Now what have you gotten started for our plan?"

"Nothing yet, damn...Russ ain't even been dead for a month yet. I don't know why you started all this bullshit so soon. You didn't even let him get in the dirt good. If you keep moving the way you movin', we gon' get caught up. Now I have some business to take care of. I'll be back later on. If that girl ain't tried to runaway yet, get her a new phone before she does and ya dumb ass be fucked!" Pete snapped before walking out of the door.

Apparently, Rose had used Essence's phone and called him on it. I wanted to fuck her up, but I was going to chill like Pete asked me to. Sometimes, he said dumb shit, but at other times, he was right. Since we had gotten this room for a whole day, I figured I would just lay around until I was ready to head home.

****

After I took my nap, I needed to meet up with the doctor that was supplying me with sleeping pills. I had been putting them in Rose's food for the past couple of weeks, and they had been working. At first, they had taken a little time to get in her system, but now, baby girl be out like a light, and it seemed like every time she woke up, she ate. I made sure to have a plate ready for her and in the microwave no matter the time of day. A tap on my window brought me out of my thoughts. I looked up and saw it was the doctor, so I hit the lock button on my car to let him in.

"Hey Constance...how are you?"

"Hey Doc...I'm good as always. Just having trouble sleeping. Did you bring me two prescriptions?"

"Yes... I brought what you asked for. You know I'm always here for you, Constance, if you ever need to talk, right?"

Me and Doctor McClain had a thing going on way back when until he married, Latisha Strong. Brian McClain played with the both of our hearts for years. I guess Latisha was doing more than me because that was who he ended up with.

"Ain't you still married, Brian?"

"Nope...she still married, but I'm not," Brian said with a straight face. I couldn't do shit but laugh; these niggas were something else no matter if they were old or young. They all were out here just trying to get their dicks wet.

"You still the same, Brian. Don't care about no one's feelings but yours. Give me what I came for so I can go. If I think about spending any time with you, I know your number."

"Alright, so make sure you use it. I could sure put your ass to sleep whether you keep taking these damn pills. Do you know how many side effects they have?"

"Listen Brian, I don't have time to be sitting here talking to you. I have to go."

He handed me the scripts then jumped out the car, and I took off. I didn't have time for his ass; I needed to get back home to keep an eye on Rose. Them stupid ass daughters of mine didn't know how to keep an eye on her.

Twenty minutes later, I was pulling up to my house, and a familiar car was sitting in my driveway. I couldn't remember whose car it was, but I was sure I had seen it before. I hurried and parked my car and got out to see who the hell these damn girls had in my fucking house. When I walked into the house, Thorne was sitting on my couch right in the middle of both my girls with his arms on them.

"Well, hello, Constance...what's good with you?" Thorne said with a dumb ass smirk on his face.

"Eboni and Essence...what is he doing in my damn house? Y'all know damn well I don't allow company in my home when I'm not home!" I snapped, and Thorne laughed.

"Constance, when you gon' take the tittie out they mouth? I came here to check on y'all like I normally do. They safe with me being here. Where's Rose at?"

"She's sleeping like always," Essence said.

"Why she sleep so much? Is she pregnant?" Thorne asked.

"I don't know, that would have to be something you have to ask her whenever she wakes."

"I think I need to go up and knock on her room door. I don't like how every time I come here, she's up in her room. Y'all sure y'all not keepin' her prisoner up in here?" Thorne chuckled while getting up and heading up my steps.

"Excuse me, Mr. Williams, where might you be going?"

"Oh...I'm just going to go check on Rose. If she cool, then you shouldn't mind me going up to check on her," he said with a straight face.

I looked over at Essence, and she nodded her head letting me know it was cool. I guess Rose's door was open, and the lock wasn't on it. I didn't know why they had opened the door, but I was happy they did. All I needed was him to see that shit, and all hell would have broken lose. I followed him up to Rose's room and just like we had told him, she was stretched across her bed still sleeping from the day before. He stood in her doorway looking around for a second. I was hoping he didn't see anything out of the ordinary.

"You see she's sleeping, now is there anything else we can help you with, Thorne?" I asked.

"Nope...you cool, but I want her to go to the doctor. Sleeping like this isn't normal unless she's sick or pregnant. I'll be back in about a week. If you don't take her to the doctor, I will," Thorne said while heading downstairs and out my front door. I didn't know what his fetish was about Rose, but I had to pay close attention to Mr. Thorne Williams.

CHAPTER 13

Honor

I hadn't seen Rose in about a week and a half, and I was starting to get worried. I hadn't even talked to her. I would text her and get no response. I would call, and I didn't get an answer, the phone just kept ringing, so I made my way over to her house. I hated these bitches including they weird ass mama. I banged on the door for what seemed like forever before someone came to answer.

"Bitch...what the fuck you doin' at my front door?" Eboni sassed as soon as she opened the door.

"Look hoe...I didn't come here to fight. I just wanted to check on Rose. I've been calling her, and she hasn't been responding. I need to make sure you hoes didn't do anything to her."

"Nobody did anything to that fat ass bitch. First, your cousin came here last week checking for her, now here you come. I wish y'all take her ugly ass to y'all house."

"Eboni...what the hell is going on out here?" Her ugly ass mama asked, coming to the door.

"This trick here looking for Rose. This is Thorne's cousin, Honor."

"I remember her from the funeral. What, he sent you here? I told that boy we were fine."

"He didn't send me here, ma'am. I came on my own, I haven't been able to reach Rose, and we usually text each other every day. I'm just here to make sure she's good."

"Well, Rose is good. I don't know why she's not responding to you, but I will let her know you came by when she wakes up," Eboni's mama said, and for some reason, I wasn't buying what she was saying. I had a feeling something was wrong. I didn't say anything, I just went to jump in my truck to make my way over to Thorne's crib. He hadn't been talking to me, but I needed to know what happened the last time he came over.

I could feel their eyes on me until I pulled off. Something was creepy about all of them, and I hope to God Rose was good. I started my truck up and peeled off with Rose on my mind.

****

I was pulling up in front of Thorne's house, and Cace was parked out front. *Oh my God, what is he doing here?* I said to myself. Cace and I had got into a big argument a couple days ago, because he was ready to tell Thorne about me and him. I wasn't ready for that though. Thorne and I were already going through issues with him thinking I'm was a kid. I got my mind situated then got out of the car. I knocked on the door, and Thorne opened it right up.

"What you doin' here, brat?" he asked.

"I just left Rose's house, and I wanted to know when you went there last week was she good? I've been texting and calling, and she haven't responded yet. I don't like this, Thorne, especially since we talk every day."

"Come on in, you and baby girl done gotten close I see."

"Yes...she's really good peoples, and I'm sorry she has been through so much. I just wanna be a good friend to her since she lost her family, you know?" I said in a serious tone.

"I know, cuz...I know... I went over there a week ago, and I talked them thots into letting me in. They so scared of they mama, so I was in shock. Once I got in, I started flirting and shit trying to ease my way on in so I could get them to tell me some shit about Rose, but Mommy Dearest walked in and fucked my plans up."

"Hey Honor...what's good with you, ma?" Cace spoke walking towards the.

"What's up...Thorne, I'm going to sit in the living room," I said, walking away.

The argument we had, he decided he didn't wanna be with me unless I told Thorne about us. I wasn't ready to do so, and I felt like if he really wanted to be with me, he would act like it and wait till I was ready. I loved him and everything, but we'd hidden it all this time, I didn't know why he just couldn't wait a little longer.

"So, this really got you messed up?" Thorne asked while sitting down in his recliner that sat across from the couch.

"Yes...I don't trust who she lives with, and her going through what she's going through doesn't make it any better."

"Well, I plan on going over there tomorrow. I told Constance that if she doesn't take Rose to the doctor, I'ma take her myself. Every time I go over there, she's sleeping, and that shit ain't cool. I got up and walked to her room last time I went over there. She was spread out across the bed knocked out. Do you think she's pregnant?" Thorne asked.

"No, she hasn't been with anyone in years. She said she did it once when she was seventeen and never did it again, and that was when she lived in Georgia. She's really an innocent girl, Thorne."

"So, her being pregnant is ruled out."

"The sleeping could be from depression. That's why I told her she needed to see someone. Talking about what she's been through may help her a lot. I'm really scared for her, Thorne, and once again, I don't trust ugly and her puppies."

"I don't trust her ass either. I been didn't trust her when Russ was living. Plus, between me and you, I've been seeing some shit that I don't like. Sooner or later though, what happens in the dark will damn sure come to the light. Enough about all of that though. I promise I'ma look into it for you, so don't stress yaself out. Now tell me what's up between Cace and you? When you see him, you usually speak and hug him just like you do me. Are y'all good?"

Damn, I had no idea we were that obvious. We needed to talk to get this crazy feeling between us out of the way before Thorne caught on. The last thing I needed him to do was catch on. I at least wanted to be out of Auntie Tina's house when I came clean about us two. Hopefully, Cace would still want me. Thinking that made sadness come over me, and all I wanted to do was go home, crawl in my bed, and cry.

"We good...I just don't feel like being bothered today. I'm so worried about Rose," I lied.

"I told you I got this. Now go home and relax. As a matter of fact, Mama said she was cooking tonight. I guess I can slide through and eat dinner with y'all. I have a couple of things to take care of, then I'll be there. Now go ahead home and relax. I got you, no matter what we go through, whenever you need me, I'll be there, OK?"

"Alright...I'll see you later, bighead." Thorne walked me to the door and stood in the doorway until I got in my car and peeled off.

CHAPTER 14

Cace

I was having a terrible day and seeing Honor at Thorne's crib made it even worse. Me and baby girl had a big argument, and we both said some things that we didn't mean--one being I didn't wanna be with her anymore. I loved her with all my heart and didn't want no one but her. I knew we were young as hell, but when you grew up before your time, you'd been there and done that. Shit I done had so many different women in my past, now I was just ready to settle down. To get my mind off some shit, I decided to take a ride around and check on a couple of the traps. Usually, that was Big Roy's job, but he had just had a baby last night, so I gave him the day off. I parked in front of our smallest trap that sat on the corner of Morse Street and Thornedike. Niggas was outside talking, smoking, and in bitch's faces like always. I parked the wheel and jumped out.

"Yo, Cace, what's good with you, my nigga?" Wiley asked while walking over to dap me up.

"Nothing much...just coming out here to check on y'all since Roy busy. How's shit going?"

"Shit good...we actually need to reup already. I hit Thorne up, and he said he got it covered. This new shit y'all got goin' on is doing numbers."

"That's what's up. How them new niggas workin' out?"

"They OK...I've been keeping a good eye on them. You know I don't do new people too well, but it's going alright. Trust me, if it was a problem, I would handle it before Roy's ass. You know he wanna talk to a nigga first and give chances. Versus me, I'll fire a nigga. Hell, I'll even shoot a mutha fucka for fucking up."

"Yeah, because ya crazy ass ain't got no chill. That's why you and Roy stayed best friends for years, y'all balance each other out, so did you see the baby yet?"

"Yup...I went to see her this morning. She's gorgeous, man. Looking just like Roy fat ass." Wiley chuckled.

"Damn, he had a girl. I couldn't imagine having a little princess!" I beamed.

"Shit, my ass don't want none. I'll be God daddy to all Roy's kids."

"Nigga, somebody gon' make you a daddy, and when that happens, that's when you gon' know you in love."

"Say what now, nigga? What the fuck is love," Wiley said causing me to chuckle.

"Yo, you funny as hell. I'm about to get out of here and go check the other traps. Then I'll probably hit the strip club up tonight if I'm not too tired."

"OK...hit me up, I'll step out with you."

"Alright...stay safe," I told Wiley while dapping him up. As soon as I hopped in my whip, I heard my phone going off. I picked it up and saw it was Thorne calling.

"Yo, where you at?"

"I just left the trap on Morse. Why, what's up?"

"Mama is cooking, and she told me to call you over."

"Ok...I'll be there after I check the other two traps. You already over there?"

"Nah...I have to get Wiley and them some more product, so I'ma be a little minute."

"Why you doin' that? Where the fuck is Pete at?"

"Man...I don't fucking know, but I'm about sick of his shit. That's a discussion for another day."

"Alright, well be careful out there, and I'll see you when you get to mama's."

Dinner at Mama Tina's house was going to be awkward, but I would be able to hold my composure. Honor was going to be the one to have the hard time. To be honest with y'all, I wish we just put this shit on the table tonight. It'd only been a couple of days, but my ass was missing her like it'd been a damn week. I was used to her staying with me some nights, and nights she didn't, we'd be on the phone all night. We got that teenage love type shit, that shit when we didn't wanna be away from each other for long. Once I was situated in the car, I peeled off and headed to my next destination.

****

"Hey baby, I'm glad you were able to come. Thorne is running late, and Honor is sleeping. You can go ahead and sit in the living room or go ahead up and wake Honor's ass up," Mama Tina said.

"Nah...I'm good with waiting in the living room until everyone is ready."

"Alright baby, you know where everything is; make yaself at home."

I was too tired to argue with Honor that's why I decided against going up to her room and waking her up. Plus, I was tired as shit, I wanted to lean my head on the back of the couch and shut my eyes for a second, even if it was only for ten minutes.

A light tap on my shoulder woke me up. I looked up, and Honor was walking away. My baby had on a sports bra and a pair of tights. I couldn't do shit but shake my head. She knew better than to walk around this house like that while I was here.

"Dinner is ready, and I wish you stop burning a hole in my damn back!" she sassed. I laughed while getting up off the couch. I ran up behind her and pulled her close to me and whispered in her ear.

"I can burn a hole in that ass anytime I feel like it," I said while grinding my middle against her ass.

"Boy...stop it before somebody sees us," Honor said while snatching away.

"Ain't nobody tell you to come down here dressed like that," I said while smacking her on the ass causing her to run away.

"Stop it, boy!" she yelled.

"What you doin' to my cousin, nigga?" Thorne asked, walking in the front door. Right then and there I wanted to say something, but the look Honor had on her face told me not to do it.

"Man...ain't nobody doing nothing to that little brat. She hit me then ran off, on some kid shit like all the time," I said, putting emphasis on kid shit. Honor rolled her eyes and made her way into the dining room where Mama Tina was waiting for us.

"Come on in here and sit down. Y'all two talk enough when you're not here. I fixed some pot roast, white rice, yams, collard greens, and corn muffins."

"Damn...Mama, that sounds good. You were in here cooking like it was Sunday."

"I've been off a couple of days, so I figured I would make y'all something to eat. Y'all be so busy in them streets, I know y'all barely get to eat a home-cooked meal. These fast ass girls that y'all be out here messing with can't cook," Mama Tina said causing us all to laugh.

"You're something else, Mama," Thorne said while shaking his head.

We all sat and ate in quiet. I could feel Honor staring at me, but every time I looked up, she would turn her head. Her ass was something else. She didn't want no one to know about us, but it was hard for her to not deal with me. I knew sooner or later, I was gon' get my baby back, and we wouldn't have to keep this shit a secret.

CHAPTER 15

Thorne

Two weeks had gone by, and I had yet to see Constance. They little asses would act like they weren't home when I would pop up over there. Then I decided to get Pete to head over there, but his lying ass would say they wasn't answering for him either. That was funny to me being as though I had found out that him and strong face had been getting it in. The fucked-up shit was I had people looking into it, and these two had been doing them for a minute which meant they were fucking around when Big Russ was living. All this shit got me wondering.

"Yo, bro, what's good with you?" Cace asked entering my office.

"Man...I promised Honor I was going to figure out what was up with Rose, but Constance and them been on the bullshit."

"Well, you know how I do. Let's go up in there with force entry since they wanna play."

"Alright, let's do this since she wanna play with me. She really doesn't know who the fuck I am, so it's time I showed her and her thot ass daughters."

I jumped up from my desk and made my way out of the door with Cace following behind me. I felt like making sure Rose was safe was my job. Her pops did everything for me and made me the man that I was today. When me and my mama didn't have, he made sure we were, on top of grooming me to take over his business.

After gathering a couple of our other men, Cace and I loaded up my 2019 Black Yukon and peeled off. Cace pulled a blunt out his pocket and sparked it up. I was shocked because it'd been a minute since I saw him spark up.

"What's on ya mind, bro?"

"Nothing, why you ask me that?"

"Because you sitting over there sparking up, and I don't remember the last time I saw you smoking. What you having relationship problems already, and I didn't even meet baby girl yet?"

"Something like that... she scared to tell her big brother about us because she only eighteen. I mean, she acts older than what she really is, and she'll be nineteen soon. I'm really feeling her, bro. I know I'm a little older than her, but shit, it's only five years."

"Man, that's a touchy situation for any brother or daddy, so I wouldn't even know what to say to that."

"What if a twenty-three-year-old wanted to talk to Honor? How would you react to that?"

"Man...I'm already tripping about everything that Honor does, so you already know how I would react, but at a point in life, I'm going to have to let baby girl do her and figure it all out on her own. I know I be hard on her right now, but I just want her to handle her business and follow her dreams. That boyfriend shit can come later," I said being honest.

"I feel you...I feel you," Cace said in deep thought.

Twenty minutes had passed, and we were pulling up to Constance's crib. The lights were on, and cars were in the driveway, so we knew someone was in the house. Me, Cace, and the two youngins I had in the backseat jumped out.

"Y'all two go around the back, and Cace and I will go through the front. Once we get in, I will give y'all the OK when we get in."

Cace and I banged on the door like we were the cops, and finally, Essence opened the door. She looked at me like she was shocked to see me this time of night.

"Can I help you?" she asked in a low tone.

"You already know what the hell I want, now where is she?" I snapped.

"Shsss...Hold on a second, and I'll be out to talk to y'all. Let me make sure Eboni is nowhere close," Essence said while going back in the house. Cace and I looked at each other curiously, but we didn't say a word. Essence walked back out and closed the door.

"Ok...so what's going on?" I asked.

"Rose is not here, and she's been gone for two days. I'm scared for her because she didn't have any money. You know Rose is not used to being out here in the streets, and she doesn't have a phone. I'm really scared for her."

"From my understanding, you don't like her, so why all the sudden you act like you care?"

"I know we didn't start out on a good note, but I don't like what my mama has been doing to her."

Hearing Essence say that had me wondering exactly what was going on. I knew her mama was on some grimy shit, but I just wasn't sure what she was up to. I gave Essence a death stare making sure to let her know I needed to hear what the fuck was going on.

"Exactly what the fuck was your mama doing to her?"

"The beatings started a couple of days after the funeral. Then she put a lock on Rose's door and kept her locked in the room. Then the last thing that I felt the need to tell Rose because I felt like my mama was doing way too much. She was putting something in Rose's food, and we think that's why she was sleeping so much. When I told Rose what was going on, she left that night and haven't been seen since."

After Essence ran everything down, my ass was furious, and when I get my hands on her ugly ass mama, she was as good as gone.

"Do you know why your mama is tripping on Rose like this?"

"I think she's pissed off because Russ didn't leave her shit; he left everything to you and Rose, but my mama told Rose that Russ took her money that her mama left her and gave everything to you. I don't think Rose believes her, but I do know that my mama probably has Rose's money."

"Where's your mama at now?" I asked.

"I don't know, maybe with one of her many dudes that she be dealing with."

"Did you tell her that Rose ran away?"

"Yes, and she said the little broke bitch will be back." My blood was boiling listening to everything that Essence had just told me. I was now on a mission to find out where the fuck Constance was, and my first stop was Pete's crib.

"Cace, get them niggas from the back, and let's get them to the warehouse. Wiley can stay there with them until I get back. Me and you have a run to make. Then when we done, we can go back to the warehouse. I need to have a meeting, I need people out in these streets looking for Rose." I thanked Essence for her services and promised her that I would hit her up when we found Rose. The thought of everything I was just told had my blood boiling. I pulled my phone out to let this fuck nigga know I was on my way. The phone rung four times before he finally picked up.

"Yo, you at the crib?"

"Yes...I just got out the shower. Are you good?"

"No...I ain't good, but I'll be there to tell you about it in about fifteen."

Soon as I hung my phone up, I peeled off and headed to drop my boys off at the warehouse, then I was going to Pete's house. I needed to see what I could get out of him since I knew he was banging Constance's back out.

CHAPTER 16

Rose

It had been the longest two days of my life. I had been laying in Farnham Park on a bench. I didn't know anything about this park, but I met up with a girl that was around my age named Meagan, and she helped me through.

"You...OK over there?" Meagan asked.

"Yes...I'm cool, I guess. I just can't believe this bitch was putting shit in my food. Like what the fuck did I do to her for her to treat me this way?"

"That bitch just wasn't right in the head, that's all, but you did the right thing getting away from her. If your dad's people are who you said they were, you won't be out here long. Why don't you have anyone's phone number."

"I just met Honor, and Constance took my phone, and I didn't have time to ask Essence for anything because I was trying to get the fuck out of there before Constance came back."

"Damn, that's fucked up," Meagan said right before a light started shining our way. She looked up with a scared look on her face. I hurried and sat up then put my book bag on my back.

"What's wrong, Meagan, is everything good?"

"No...it's Razor, and he's a pimp. Go and run to the back of the park in the little hut back there. I'll talk to him."

"Meagan...I'm not going to leave you here. You have been helping me, and you don't even know me. The least I could do is stay here with you."

"No...please go, you're not cut out for this. Plus, you're beautiful, and you're new meat out here in these streets. He would have a ball if he saw you, so go. I've been with him before, I'll just runaway again when the time is permitted. It was nice meeting you, Rose, and I pray you find your family soon. Now please go...please go," Meagan pleaded, and she didn't have to tell me twice.

I ran to the back of the park like she told me to. It was dark as fuck back here, but no one could see me. I curled up in the corner and covered up with my blanket. I didn't know shit about being out here on these streets, so I was definitely going to stay out here until it was daylight. Which would be soon since it was wee hours of the morning.

****

"Yo, Thorne, over here." A sound of someone screaming woke me up. I had been sleep for maybe an hour or so. I was so scared out here, but I knew I needed to close my eyes for a second. I pulled the blanket from over my face and saw three dudes standing in front of me.

"Little Rose...is that you?" Pete asked, walking up. I jumped up and ran over to him, and he pulled me in for a hug. The tears started falling from my eyes as soon as he pulled me.

"I was so scared...I had to get away," I cried out.

"You're going to be ok, baby girl," Pete assured me.

"Hey...lil' mama, you good? Did anyone touch you?" Thorne asked.

"No...please just get me out of here."

Thorne and Pete looked me over to make sure I was good then they walked me over to a black truck. I didn't know where they were taking me, but I hoped it wasn't back to Constance's house.

"Where too?" Cace asked.

"We takin' her to my mama's with Honor."

"Don't we need to let Constance know she's good?" Pete asked.

"Fuck no, we don't need to let that bitch know shit. She needs to go to my mama's house with Honor like I said, end of discussion!" Thorne snapped, and everyone moved on command. I didn't know what was going to come of my life, but I was happy as hell I didn't have to spend another night in the streets. The whole time the truck was moving, I looked out the window in deep thought. I was wondering if I would ever catch a break.

About fifteen minutes went by, and Thorne was dropping his crew off. After everyone was out of his truck, he jumped in the driver seat and peeled off.

"You good back there, ma?"

"Yes...just a little hungry and tired."

"OK, cool...we can stop by the store to get you some food, then I'll take you to Honor. Chinese, Spanish, or Jamaican food, which one do you want?"

"Spanish food is fine," I assured him.

Thorne had stopped and gotten me some roasted chicken, yellow rice, kidney beans, and sweet plantains. Now we were pulling up in front of his mama's house. Before I even got out, Honor was running out of the front door. She opened up the door and helped me out of the truck.

"Oh, my God...Rose I was so worried about you," she said while pulling me in for a hug. I hugged her back, and once again, the tears started to fall."

"I miss you too...I thought I was never going to see you again."

"Well, Thorne told me he was going to find you for me, and that's exactly what he did. I can't wait to see ya step mama. I wanna beat that ugly bitch's ass so bad."

"Well, how about we jump her?" I giggled, causing Honor to laugh at me. Me and her walked into the house. Thorne grabbed my bookbag, and the food he had just purchased.

"Mama...I bought y'all something to eat since I had to get Rose something!" Thorne yelled out.

"Thank you, baby...I'll be down in a minute."

"Alright, y'all two, I'm out. I have some business to take care of. If either of you need me for anything, be sure to hit my phone up."

"Thorne...it's one thing I want to ask of you. If you can't, that's fine, but I won't be able to sleep until I ask."

"Ok, lil' mama, what's on your mind?"

"There was a girl who stayed in the park with me the two nights I was out there. Her name was Meagan Greene. Last night, a pimp named Razor was skimming the park for new girls. She told me to run and leave her. I didn't want to, but she assured me that she would be fine. She didn't want Razor to see me because I was new, and he would have been in heaven. If you know anything about Razor, can you please find her and get her from there?"

"I got you, lil' mama," Thorne said before heading out the door.

"So, talk to me...are you good?" Honor asked.

"No, not really, but one day, I'll be OK. I'm just glad to be out of that house."

"Hello baby...I'm Mama Tina, Thorne's mama. How are you feeling?"

Thorne's mama was so beautiful with her chocolate skin and long hair. Thorne looked a lot like her, he was just a little lighter. When she first walked in the room, I thought to myself, *Damn, that's where he gets his looks from.*

"I'm OK...just hungry and tired."

"OK...well go ahead and shower while I heat this food up a little. When you finished, come on in the dining room and we can all eat lunch together. You're welcome to stay as long as you want. My babies seem to be worried about your well-being, which means you're a good person. Not to mention your father was a good man, and my home will always be opened to you," Mama Tina assured me.

"OK, and thank you so much, ma'am."

"Come on, I'll show you where everything is," Honor said while grabbing my hand. I walked through the house and up the steps. The house was beautiful, and Ms. Tina kept it nice. She had pictures all over the place of Thorne and Honor when they were little. I even saw a couple of pictures of Cace and Thorne. They were so damn cute when they were little. When we made it to Honor's bedroom, she gave me a clean towel and wash cloth then walked me to the bathroom.

"My Bluetooth speaker was already in there, is there any specific music you would like to listen to?"

"Can you please put on Pandora? I love 702's station."

"Yesss...that's my shit," Honor cooed.

Once the music was on and I turned the water to the temperature I liked, I jumped right in. There was soap, shampoo, and conditioner already in here. I let the water run down on my body starting from the top of my head. This very moment, I hoped and prayed that today started off to a better life for me. It seemed like my shit went from sugar to shit in no time, and I needed a break. I was too young to be dealing with all of this.

CHAPTER 17

Constance

The past couple of days I had been hiding out. Word on the street was that Thorne had been looking for me. I knew that fat bitch had made her way over to them people. As soon as I got my fucking hands on her again, it was going to be all over. Pete had been calling me off the hook, and I didn't wanna talk to his ass because I knew he was going to tell me what I shouldn't and should have been doing. I didn't wanna hear that shit.

"What you in here thinking about?"

"Just a little pissed off about how everything is going down. If Pete's punk ass would have hurried and got rid of Thorne's ass, everything would be cool. All he had to do was end his life right after Russ died, and it would have looked like both murders were involved."

"I been told you not to fuck with his punk ass. Shit, I told you not to fuck with Russ' bitch ass too, but nah, the money blinded you. Now look, that nigga didn't leave you shit," Dom stressed.

Dominick Lewis and Peter Collins were both Russ' boys. They had been down with Russ when he first started the empire. I wasn't around back then, but when I first met them both, they seemed like some legit friends until they both wanted a piece of the pie, which was me. See, Russ made sure they were paid good, but they both had gotten greedy. They noticed Russ training the younger niggas hard, and that's when they came to the conclusion that he wasn't leaving the empire to either one of them which made them both vengeful. I got why Russ was doing it the way he was doing it. He didn't want what he worked so hard for to get ran down in the ground because of Pete and Dom. Neither of them were made to be the boss. Dom had gambling issues versus Pete just wasn't hard enough if you ask me. How I got close to the both of them was crazy. I would use them both in different ways. Like Pete ran his mouth like a bitch, so I always knew when Russ was out here cheating on me. Then Dom had big dreams of taking over the empire then me and him riding off into the sunset. I had other plans though. I wanted them to get rid of Thorne then I would have them at each other's neck to the point somebody was going to kill somebody. I had everything all mapped out.

"Dom...I don't feel like hearing all that shit right now. I'm already pissed off that the little bitch got away."

"What the fuck is your problem with that little girl? All you had to do was give her the share of the money and let her go back to Georgia. She doesn't like you, and you don't like her, so she wasn't coming the fuck back. Ya dumb ass just don't listen. Just starting shit for no reason."

"That little bitch and her mama always were in the way of my marriage being fucked up."

"Well, you knew when you married that nigga he was still in love with Lela. Always was, shit he only got with you to take his mind off her, and the shit never worked."

"He had to have some love for me because he married me."

"Nope, none at all...he just did that because he was getting old and didn't wanna play out here in these streets. He even went to Lela and gave her an ultimatum; either they were getting back together, or he was marrying you, so that was just to get under Lela's skin. Neither one of them made any sense because they still continued to deal with each other." I stared at Dom with my nose turned up. I couldn't believe he was sitting here talking about all this dumb ass shit that he knew would piss me the hell off.

"That's why I took care of that stupid bitch!" I snapped, not meaning to let that cat out of the bag.

"Tell me you didn't do that shit, Constance. I can't believe ya ass, that shit was not in the plans. What the fuck is wrong with you? You make shit hard for yourself. This shit here was one of the reasons you should have let baby girl go off to Georgia and leave here. All this shit is going to backfire in your face. I'm out of here, you do way too much," Dom bitched while walking out of the door.

I didn't care how he felt. I did what I did to get what I wanted. When Lela died, something in my head triggered. I, for once in my life, could tell how much he loved her. I had to sit and watch my man grieve over another bitch; the shit almost killed me. Then when he took Rose in instead of letting her live with her grand mom, the shit pissed me off. All he kept saying was Lela didn't fuck with her mama, so he didn't want his daughter over there. Everything was always about what Lela wanted. My mind drifted off to the day I went to pay Ms. Lela a visit.

The girls and I had made it to Georgia a couple days ago. I had Russ thinking I came down here to look at a new school for Eboni since she wanted to go to school to be a fashion designer. I had heard Clark Atlanta was a good school for that. I had dropped

Eboni and Essence off at the hotel then made my way to see Lela. I had heard Russ talking to Pete a while back telling him how Lela had heart problems. So, I had called Brian and had him make me up something to shoot in her arm that could cause her to have a heart attack. Then they wouldn't have thought of foul play at all since the hoe already had a bad heart.

After making sure the girls were cool, I made my way to Lela's home. I jumped out of the rental that I was driving and knocked on her door. She opened on the third knock.

"Well hello, Constance, what brings you over? I know Russ told me you were coming to town to check out the school for the girls. It's a real good school."

"Aww...thanks so much, that's good to hear, but I wanted to talk to you woman to woman. Can I please come in?"

"Sure...come on in," Lela said, not expecting a thing.

"This is a nice place you have here. Where is Rose at?" I asked, not really giving a damn.

"She's at her little girlfriend's house. Would you like something to drink before we get started?"

"Nah...I'm good. I just wanted to know when are you going to stop fucking Russ, that's all."

"Wait...what did you just say to me?"

"Bitch, you heard me. When are you going to stop fucking my man?"

"Constance...I know good and got damn well you didn't come all the way over here to ask me some dumb shit like that. Does Russ know you were coming the hell over here on good bullshit? We are too old for this shit. Not to mention this should have been something you asked your husband instead of bringing this bullshit to my house."

I was growing tired of her steady talking but not answering my damn question. I jumped on her ass, and we began to fight like teenage girls. Yeah, the shit was immature, but I didn't give a damn; I wanted her to leave my man the fuck alone. I didn't wanna put any marks on Lela, so I let her hit me a couple of times before I took the syringe from my purse and shot her in the neck. I didn't know what Brian put in the syringe, but her ass started grabbing her chest like she was having a heart attack. I just sat and watched her until she took her last breath. I checked her pulse then looked her body over to make sure nothing was out of place then made my way out of the door before Rose walked in.

That day was so crazy, I had a little bruise on my face that makeup could cover, and then I made my way back to the hotel with the girls. I couldn't rush home because I had to make the shit believable. When Rose had gotten home later that night, she found her mama on the floor dead. Russ called and asked me to go there and be there for his daughter until he could make it down there. I did as I was told like the good wife and watched this bitch ass nigga cry all fucking night. He even stayed in Atlanta for a while before he came back with Rose. He made the funeral arrangements, and he paid for everything. Come to find out, he was still this bitch's power of attorney. Right then and there, I realized how much I was starting to hate my husband.

CHAPTER 18

Honor

Today was my birthday party, and Thorne and Auntie Tina had gone all out like always. Of course, I was late as hell for my own party. You know me, I had to make a grand entrance.

"Girl, if you look in that mirror one more time, you look pretty, Rose," I assured her.

"I'm sorry, it's just that I never wore make up before."

"Well baby, you look good as hell today, and I be seeing you checking out my cousin, what's that all about?"

"Just like I be seeing you eyeing Cace. When y'all gon' stop playing and get back together or whatever y'all call it?"

"Whatever, come on before Thorne call me again."

I looked around the parking lot of Club Trinity, and it was filled to the compacity. I didn't know who all Thorne invited, but the city had definitely come out for your girl. I grabbed Rose's hand, and we walked in the door. As soon as we made it to the VIP section, which was half of the fucking club. I looked around in "aww" my cousin had really showed up and showed out for me. Everything was decorated in my favorite colors, purple, white and gold. The way the club was set up, it looked like a hall with decorated tables and centerpieces. I swear he did the hell out of this. I didn't know who he hired to decorate, but whoever they were, they did the damn thing.

"The lady of the night has arrived, so let's get this party started. Everybody, please give the birthday girl, Honor, a round of applause. Then, *Birthday Bitch* by. *Trap Beckham* blared through the speakers.

"One time for the birthday bitch,
Two times for the birthday bitch,
Three times for the birthday bitch,
Fuck it up if it's your birthday, bitch."

Everybody had formed a circle around me, and I started tearing it up. I could dance my ass off, and tonight, I was going to have the time of my life. It had been a rough month, and Cace and I still hadn't gotten back together. I was missing him like crazy, and tonight I thought I was going to have to reveal to my cousin and auntie what the deal was. I loved Cace too much, and I needed him like I needed the air I breathed. Today when I started school, he sent me a text wishing me a good day, and right then and there, he had been on my mind for the rest of the day. The song had gone off, and everyone started hugging me and telling me happy birthday. My auntie was on her way over to me. I knew this wasn't her scene, so she was just probably coming to tell me bye.

"Look at you, beautiful. You know this ain't me, so I came to tell you happy birthday. Have a good time, and stay out of trouble."

"Thank you, Auntie Tina, I love you so much." I kissed her cheek, and she headed out the door. I looked down at my dress and admired how beautiful it was. I had on a sequin strapless, mermaid, v neck, backless gown that was lavender and a pair of silver strappy heels that came from DSW. Yeah, I liked expensive shit, but if I could find something cheap and make it look good, then that's what I was going to do. My outfit looked expensive, but it really wasn't.

"Hey cuz...you look great, baby girl," Thorne said while pulling me in for a hug.

"Thank you, where is Cace at?"

"He comin', he had to do something for me. Come on over here so I can get you and shy girl something to drink," Thorne said talking about Rose.

I looked over at her, and she was sitting at the table looking all crazy. Rose looked really pretty today. She had on a pink body con dress with a hole on the stomach, with a pair of gold strappy sandals also from DSW. She was trying not to wear it, but I told her how pretty she looked in it. I also told her how sometimes I wished my skinny ass had some curves. I beat her face to the gawds and fluffed out her naturally curly hair.

"Stop calling her names, you know she ain't used to all of this."

"I know, I like how innocent she is."

"Mmm...I know, I could tell," I sassed while rolling my eyes.

"What's that supposed to mean?" he asked, giving me the side eye.

"Umm...nothing, but Kreesha walkin' up. I didn't know you invited her."

"I didn't...her ass been blowing me the fuck up like crazy, and I've been busy. She must have heard about the party from the hood."

"I'm sure she did, but give me Rose's drink, and you go handle that," I told him while walking away. When I got over to Rose, I handed her the cup and then sat down.

"Are you good, boo?" I asked.

"Yes...I'm fine. Everything looks nice in here, and you look so beautiful."

"Well, thank you! You look beautiful too."

"Thank you so much for everything you've been doing for me. I really appreciate you, it's like you fell right out of the sky right when I needed you. Now we two peas in a pod," Rose said with a huge smile on her face.

"Alright...alright...enough of the mushy shit, let's go tear this dance floor up," I said while grabbing Rose's hand and heading to the dance floor. I was dancing all the way to the dance floor. My song had already been playing for a little minute. My part was about to come up, and I needed to be on the dance floor.

"Press, press, press, press, press,
Cardi don't need more mess,
Kill'em all, put then hoes to rest,
Walk in, bullet proof vest,
Please tell me who she gone check..."

I danced around in front of Rose while moving my hands and singing *Press* by. *Cardi B.* Everybody who knew me, knew I loved Cardi with all my heart. She was my sister in my head.

Rose and I danced and laughed through two more songs before we decided to go back to the VIP section. I was having a good time, and I needed another drink. Once we made it back up to the section, Cace was sitting down talking to some chick, but when he saw me, he got straight up. He walked over to me and pulled me in for a hug.

"Happy birthday, beautiful, and you look good as fuck in that dress," He whispered in my ear. I could tell he was already intoxicated because I could smell the Henny and weed on his breath.

"Would you stop before Thorne sees us," I said while snatching away. Cace moved and held his hands up in the air as if he was surrendering. He then went back over to the chick he was talking to and sat back down. I got annoyed instantly, and Rose pulled me to another table.

"Aht, Aht...this is not what you gon' do today. How you gon' get mad and you pushed him away?" Rose chastised. She was right, I wasn't going to show my ass today. It was my day, and I was supposed to be enjoying myself.

"Hey, beautiful...I see you enjoying yourself. You done bought the whole damn city out tonight I see." Quan walked over to Rose and me.

"Hello stranger, I haven't saw you since I beat the shit out of your baby mama a month ago. That bitch ain't here today, ready for round two is she?" I giggled while he shook his head.

"Nah...I came out dolo, ma. What you and ya girl drinkin'?"

"We good, my cousin got us all types of drinks over there."

"Damn...you always givin' a nigga a hard time," Quan stressed.

"That's because I'm too pretty to be getting into fights, and your girl already feelin' like we got something goin' on. To be honest, I'm sick of fighting her dumb ass. Now, if you excuse me, I got some partying to do," I said, feeling a little tipsy.

"Wait...at least take your card, lil' lady," Quan said, handing me a card that I was sure was full of money. I snatched it out of his hand then Rose and I headed back down to the dance floor. As we were walking away. I felt eyes on me; I looked up, and it was Cace. I looked at him and rolled my eyes.

******

The party was officially over, and it was two-thirty in the morning. Rose and I stood outside waiting for

Thorne to come out. He had told us not to move. Everybody kept walking by hugging and still saying happy birthday like we weren't on the next day of the calendar.

"This party was everything, lil' sis," Wiley, one of Thorne's boys, walked up to me and hugged me.

"Thank you, Wiley. I'm glad you made it out tonight."

"You know I wouldn't have missed it for the world."

A group of niggas walked out of the club, and I knew it was my cousin and his crew. They all stopped in front of us just talking and planning to hit the diner since we all were hungry.

"Y'all ready to go, cuz? We about to hit the diner up. You and Rose gon' ride with Cace and I. I'ma make sure they keep an eye out on your car. We will pick it up in the morning."

I shook my head at Thorne letting him know I was fine with that. I was getting dizzy, and I needed to sit my drunk ass down. We all walked over to Thorne's trunk and jumped right in. As soon as we were about to pull off the sound of gun shots were heard.

Pow...pow...pow... pow...

Gun shots riddled the side of Thorne's truck. Cace and Thorne pulled their guns out and started shooting back. The rest of the team that was left out there started shooting too.

"OUCH, SHIT!" I yelled out in pain.

"Oh, my God, Thorne...she was hit; its blood everywhere!" Rose yelled out just before everything went black.

CHAPTER 19

Cace

Hearing Rose yell out that Honor had been hit caused me to jump in the back seat to see if my baby was ok. She was knocked out and it was so much blood, I couldn't see where she was hit. She was intoxicated so I knew that was what could have been making her bleed so much. Then her passing out could have come from shock.

"Fuck...Fuck...Fuck," Thorne yelled out while banging his hands on the steering wheel.

"Bro...calm down and just get us to the hospital. She still has a strong pulse so she's fine. Just hurry up and get there." I assured Thorne to try to ease his anger a little.

"Is she going to be ok...I'ma need her to be ok." Rose cried out.

"She gone be good Rose...she gone be just fine ma." I assured her to also ease her mind a little.

I put pressure on the wound and held my baby all the way to the hospital. After Thorne broke every traffic violation, we were now pulling into Cooper Hospitals parking lot. Once the car stopped, I jumped out and carried Honor in bridal style. Once I walked in everyone started running towards me.

"What happen?" The nurses that were walking towards me asked.

"She got shot at the club. Her pulse is still strong, but there's a lot of blood. I put pressure on it the whole way here. Her name is Honor Williams and she just turned 19 yesterday."

"Ok sir...thanks a lot. What is your relationship to the patient?" The nurse asked as soon as Thorne walked in.

"She's my girl." I said not caring how Honor or Thorne felt at this very moment. They rushed her to the back on a gurney. I felt Thorne burning a hole in the side of my face, so I figure I would walk over to him and say something.

"What the fuck was that all about?" Thorne snapped.

"Man chill out it's not that serious. Honor and I been dealing with each other for over a year now. She kept it a secret because she didn't want you overreacting."

"Overreacting, huh? You mean to tell me that my little cousin is the chick that you been keeping hidden." Thorne raised his voice.

"Look nigga don't me yelling at me like that. This is not the time or place to even be talking about this." I barked.

"Nigga you better lower ya fucking tone." Thorne said while walking in my face.

"You two need to cut it out. Honor would not want this." Rose said while standing in between us.

"Oh my God...how's my baby? Where is she?" Mama Tina asked while running in the hospital.

"Mama," Thorne said while running over to his mama and pulling her in his arms.

"What the fuck happened, Thorne? I told you to watch her."

"I know, Mama...it's not my fault we were leaving the club and gunfire went off."

"Hello everyone, I'm Dr. Jiles, and who's the guardian of Honor Williams?"

"I am, sir...how is she doing?"

"Ms. Williams is fine she was only hit in the shoulder. All the blood must have come from her alcohol intake. Then she passed out from shock. Right now, one of my colleagues is in there removing the bullet and patching her up. We would like to monitor her for just one night. So, when she's finished getting fixed up, I'll come out to get you guys."

"Ok...doc thanks so much."

"Cace you can leave and take Rose home." Thorne ordered. I looked at him like he had lost his damn mind.

"Nigga...I ain't going a damn place until I see my girl." I retorted.

"She is not your fucking girl and like I said you can go."

"Thorne! If you don't cut it out in here. This is not the time or place for this. You're not the only one that loves Honor. You don't even know if Rose wants to leave. So, sit the hell down and shut up."

"Mama...this nigga been messing with Honor for a year now and didn't tell anybody."

"So, what Honor is grown now and she has to make decisions on her own." Mama Tina fussed.

"You ok with this? Let me find out you already knew." Thorne chided.

"As a matter of fact, I did. They didn't know I knew though." Mama Tina sassed.

"And you didn't tell me mama. What type shit is that?" Thorne grimaced.

"Thorne, I think you need to leave I'll tell Honor to call you when she wakes up. Because you ain't about to be making a scene in here. Plus, if you curse at me one more time you gone need a fucking doctor. Rose you look tired baby you can go ahead to Thorne's house with him and I'll have Honor to call you when she wakes up." Mama Tina said.

Rose looked like she didn't wanna go but she also looked like she was tired as fuck. So, I knew she wasn't going to oblige. Thorne looked like he was about to say some slick shit, until Rose walked over to him and grabbed his hand.

"Come on Thorne maybe we should go. Honor is ok and I'm sure she'll call us when she wakes up." Rose said in a low tone. Thorne look at her and turned to walk away. He didn't say bye or anything to me or his mama, so I knew he was pissed.

"Just give him some time and he'll be alright."

"So, how long did you know about Honor and me?" I asked curious.

I see how you two interact around each other. Then all the sudden it stopped. Not to mention at dinner the way you two kept looking at each other when y'all thought wasn't nobody watching y'all. I'm shock Thorne didn't notice it. I got one request and one request only. If you don't mean her no good Cace leave her the fuck alone. Because if you think Thorne will fuck you up, you have no idea what I'll do. Honor is a good girl and she deserves someone that's going to be good to her. I may not agree with it because of your age difference, but I know I won't be able to stop y'all. Are y'all using protection?" She asked shocking the hell out of me.

"Yes, Mama Tina and Honor is on birth control. When we first started, we went to Plan Parenthood together."

"Ok...y'all better be using something and you better remember what the hell I said."

An hour later the doctor came back out to let us know that Honor was woke and asking for her family.

Me and Mama Tina headed to the back to see her. The minute I got in the room I ran over to the bed and kissed her forehead.

"Cace, what are you doing?" Honor said once she saw her aunt walk in the room behind me.

"Baby...it's fine she already knows."

"Yup...I already know about y'all hot asses, so you can stop putting on a front. Because you real bad at it. Now how's my baby doing?" Ms. Tina asked.

"I'm fine Auntie just in a little pain. Where's Rose and Thorne?"

"Thorne was pissed because he just found out you and Cace have been sneaking behind our backs. Don't get alarmed you know how your cousin is and he will get over it. As for me I knew already and I already warned Cace's ass. Any sign of him not treating you like you should be treated leave his ass, and I'm not playing with you Honor. You know how you were raised and we in a no fuckboy zone over here."

I couldn't do shit but laugh at Ms. Tina she was something else, but I loved her just like she was my mama. We sat and talked to Honor until she fell asleep.

"Ms. Tina I'm going to head out, please tell her when she wakes up in the morning, I'll be here to pick her up."

"No baby...I'm going to go. You stay here with your girl and remember everything I told you." She kissed Honor on the cheek and made her way out of the door. I sat and watched my baby sleep everybody knowing that we were a couple now felt good. I knew my bro was mad, but I had to let that shit out it had been weighing heavy on my heart.

CHAPTER 20

Thorne

Tonight, had been a night full of surprises. First my cousin gets shot then I find out my right hand is creeping with my little cousin. I'm so fucking pissed I'm about ready to go paint this whole fucking city red. I had already been dressed in my all black and pacing the floor. Not know the first place to start. I pulled my phone out and dialed Pete's number and he picked up on the second ring.

"Yo, young blood...How's Honor doing?"

"She good, but we need to know who did this shit Pete. My truck is out front looking like a piece of swiss cheese. So, I knew that shit was meant for me. They almost killed my fucking cousin man."

"I understand why your angry, but you need to chill out tonight. You know them cops is gone be out there like crazy. Just chill til the morning and if you want, I can arrange a meeting with the team, so we can discuss getting to these streets to find out who did this."

"Man...I don't know why I even called ya ass. I should have went with my first instinct and called Dom. He would have been down for whatever. Bye nigga I'm out." I yelled into the phone right before I hung it up.

I was so angry I didn't know how to calm myself the fuck down. I felt like I was being stared at, and that's when I realized that I wasn't in my home alone. I turned around and Rose was standing right there.

"Are you ok?" She asked in a soft tone like always.

"No...I'm not my cousin got shot and I don't know who did it. Her and my right hand have been fucking around. How the fuck do you think I feel?" I snapped causing Rose to storm off. I felt bad after I did that shit, so I went to apologize. When I made it to my living room, she was lying on my couch with a throw blanket over her legs. I walked over to her and lifted her legs up so I could sit down. I placed her legs on my lap and she tried to get up.

"You good lil' mama, you don't have to move. What you in here watching?"

"I'm watching The Wood. I love this movie."

"I love it too; do you mind if I watch it with you?"

"No...this is your house Thorne. You can do whatever you want." She sassed.

"I'm sorry for talking to you like that."

"It's whatever I just know next time not to overstep my boundaries. I was just trying to help. I know your mad, but Honor is fine it's no need to go after who did this. I know I don't know much about the street life, but what I do know is that's what took my daddy away from me. None of this shit is worth you being taken away from Honor or ya mama. Just my thoughts." This was the most I ever heard her ass talk and she really did have a point, but I wasn't going to listen to her of course. I will stay in the crib with her tonight, so she won't be alone, but I knew after tonight I was going to get to the bottom of this shit.

"You right lil' mama. I'ma just stay in and watch this movie with you." I took my black Timberland boots, and my black hoodie off so I could get comfortable on the couch next to Rose. We were just about in the middle of the movie, and I could tell from Rose's eyes that she was good and tired. So, I doubt that she was going to make it to the end of the movie. Hell, as tired as I was, I may not make it, but the way my mind was going I doubt if I was going to get any sleep.

****

"Wake up Rose, I got you something to eat ma." I said while tapping Rose on the shoulder to wake her up. When I woke up the sun was shining through the window. I was shock my ass even went to sleep, but my mind was on a hundred when I woke up. I had to go out for a gym run. I needed to lift some weights and release some of this stress. While I was out, I called Dom, Pete, and Wiley to set an afternoon meeting up. Then I made my way to get Rose something to eat. I even talked to Honor she was ok, but I still was mad at her little ass. After I made sure she was straight, I told her I would bring Rose over there when I was on my way to the meeting.

"She stared up at me with one eye open and one closed."

"Hey...what time is it?"

"About 9:30, I stepped out and went to the gym, then I stopped to get you something to eat. I grabbed French toast, cheese eggs, pancakes, turkey bacon, turkey sausage, and pork bacon."

"Thorne, why did you get all of that?"

"Because I didn't know what you ate, so I bought options baby." I chuckled, watching Rose like a hawk as she sat up. Even with her hair all over the place she was still so fucking beautiful.

"How's Honor? Did she call yet?" Rose asked in one breath.

"Yeah, she's good baby girl. I told her I would take you there when I'm on my way out for my meeting."

"Ok cool...can I get a clean washcloth, towel, and a toothbrush?"

"Everything is in the guest bathroom. I left it there in case you got up. I left a clean t-shirt and some sweats up there too."

"Alright... thank you so much Thorne, for everything."

"I keep telling you no thanks needed. Now hurry up so you can eat."

While Rose was in the shower, I headed to my bedroom so I could get in the shower since I had just came from the gym. I knew after she ate, I was going to have to head to my meeting. I made my way into the bathroom and turned the shower on to the temperature I like. I then stripped out of my clothes then jumped in. After letting the water run down on my body for a little while I went ahead and washed a couple of times. Once I was satisfied, I got out dried off a little then headed into my room. Rose little ass startled me and my towel fell straight to the floor. The way she was staring at my dick caused my shit to brick right the fuck up. I couldn't do shit but shake my head. I leaned down and picked my towel up and rewrapped it back around my waist. Rose was still standing there staring like she didn't know what to say.

"What you need ma?" I asked while smiling at her.

"I'm so sorry Thorne I didn't know you were in the shower. I couldn't find you so I assumed you were in here. You didn't have the door shut, so I thought I could come right in. I'ma just go ahead downstairs and wait for you to come down."

"You good ma...we both grown. You don't have to run away you already saw my dick."

"No, I'll just go back downstairs and wait for you to come." Rose said then ran out of my room quick as hell. This little lady is really different then what I'm usually attracted too. I don't know what it is about her little sexy ass that has me so intrigued. I hurried and through some clothes on then headed down to the kitchen where Rose was eating. When I got in the kitchen Rose looked up at me then hurried and put her head back down. I walked over to her and grabbed her hand then helped her out of the seat she was sitting in. I raised her chin making sure we were looking eye to eye.

"You don't have to be scared to be around me beautiful. I won't bite unless you want me to." I said while leaning down to kiss her lips. To my surprise she kissed me right back. What was just supposed to be a little peck to see where her head was at turned into a whole tongue locking session. That I must say was amazing. I remember Honor telling me that she wasn't a virgin, but it had been a couple of years since she had did anything, so I knew it was some young love shit. Rose finally pulled away and looked at me with them sad eyes.

"Thorne...what are we doing? You know you're not interested in a girl like me, so why would you kiss me?"

"How you know what I'm interested in baby girl?"

"Thorne for one you're older than me, two I'm not the model type chick like the girl that was following you around the club last night. Look at me Thorne I'm a little over the size limit you street niggas like."

"Rose cut that dumb shit out ma. You're beautiful and I love everything about them thick thighs and all that ass." I smiled while licking my lips.

"Whatever Thorne, now let me use your phone to call Honor."

"Here, and I'ma stop and we gone get you a phone before I drop you off. I need to have a way to contact you when I'm not around.

Rose and I sat at the table and ate some of the food I brought. Whatever we didn't eat I bagged it up and would be dropping it off for all the homeless people that stay under the 10th Street bridge.

CHAPTER 21

Rose

"So, how are you feeling?" I asked while puffing up Honor's pillows while she laid in her bed.

"I'm in pain, but I'm OK. I'm a little pissed off because this is going to stop me from starting school when I'm supposed to."

"Honor...your health is more important, babes," I assured her.

"I know it is, but it's still fucked up how this all went down. They don't even know who did this or what it's pertaining to. What the fuck if it happens again?"

"It's not going to happen again, and everything is going to be just fine. Try not to worry."

"So, how was your night with my cousin's evil ass?" Honor asked.

"He tried it a couple of times with his anger issues, then he was fine. We watched TV together until we fell asleep then he went to get us some breakfast. After breakfast, I saw him naked, and we kissed," I said it fast, hoping the shit went right over her head.

"Don't be trying to talk all fast thinking I missed what you just said. How the hell did you see him naked?"

"I was running into his room to ask could I use his phone, and I scared the shit out of him, and his towel fell straight to the floor. I was all staring, practically drooling. I apologized then went back to the kitchen to eat. When he came downstairs, he lifted my head up by my chin and made sure I was looking him straight in his eyes. Then he kissed me."

"And what did you do?" Honor asked.

"I kissed him back. I don't know what came over me, but him kissing me turned me on. After we shared a passionate kiss for what seemed like forever, I had finally pulled away, and then that's when I asked him what we were doing. I told him he knows damn well he don't want a girl like me. I'm nothing like the model-looking chick that was following him around the club."

"Girl bye...you are beautiful, and Kreesha ain't no damn body. Just some thot he was fucking. You better stop feeling like you're not beautiful because of your size. My cousin really likes you; I could tell the way he looks at you. Then when he was out there searching for you in them streets confirmed it also. You may be younger than him, but I feel like age ain't nothing but a number, and plus, nobody said y'all have to get into something right now. Y'all could take things slow and just be friends. I knew something was up when he bought you that new phone. That nigga thinks he slick--he wanna keep tabs on you."

"Shut up, Honor. He is not trying to keep no tabs on me. Men like Thorne don't get involved with girls like me," I assured her. A knock at her room door brought us out of our conversation. I went to open it so she wouldn't have to move. When I opened the door, Thorne was standing right there.

"Why haven't you sent me your new number yet?" he asked as soon as I opened the room door.

"I didn't set it up yet. I've been in here talking to Honor. Why, is there a reason you rushing me?"

"Come downstairs and holla at me for a minute," Thorne demanded, and the shit made me aroused. I told Honor I would be back, and I followed him downstairs. Once we made it to the living room, Thorne got all up in my space, causing my heart to beat fast.

"What do you want, Thorne?"

"I've been thinking about you like crazy since we kissed earlier."

"So, and what's that supposed to mean?"

"I want you, Rose, and I've noticed you want me too, but ya shy ass isn't going to admit it. It's cool though, because I always get what I want."

"Mmm...so you want me, huh?"

"Yup, and real soon, you gon' be mine. I got some shit to take care of, but I'll be back in about an hour. Be dressed, I wanna take you out to eat. Oh yeah and hurry up and hook that phone up so we can text," Thorne demanded and walked out of the door. I couldn't believe him, all we did was share a kiss, and this nigga just thought he was my man already.

I headed back upstairs to tell Honor what happened, but she was sound asleep, so I looked through my book bag and pulled out a pair of black distressed jeans and a red crop top shirt that said, 'My black is beautiful'. It was cute, but I still wasn't sure if I wanted to wear it. Honor had bought it for me when we went shopping for her birthday party. I looked through the book bag and didn't see anything else that would look right with the jeans. I just said fuck it and topped the outfit off with a pair of red and white Vans. After everything was laid out, I sat on the bed and started messing with the phone to get it hooked up. Thoughts of all the shit I had at my daddy's house came to mind. I needed to go there and get my shit. I made a mental note to get Thorne to go there to get my things.

"What you sitting there thinking about?" Honor asked bringing me out of my thoughts.

"While you were sleep, I was trying to find something to wear. Then I thought about all the shit I had at my daddy's house. I need my shit."

"Your man gon' make sure you get a new wardrobe, girl. Fuck that shit you got over there."

"Now here you go. I don't have a man."

"Well, what did he say that he had to pull you in another room?"

"Get my phone set up and he'll be back in an hour to pick me up for dinner, so get dressed."

"Well, get ya ass up and go get dressed. I see your clothes laid out already. You talk all that shit, and you know you gon' do everything he said do," Honor said, and I stuck my tongue out at her and made my way into the bathroom. She was right, my ass was going to do exactly what Thorne said. Shit, I was hungry.

An hour and a half later, I was in the car with Thorne, and we were pulling up at Red Lobster. After he parked, he got out and walked around to the passenger side to open the door for me. Thorne put his hand out to grab mine helping me out of the car. I couldn't do shit but smile. He was being such a gentleman and I was loving every bit of it.

****

Now we were sitting in the restaurant, talking and laughing while we were waiting for our food. I couldn't deny the way I was feeling right now if I tried. Thorne had me feeling better than I had in a long time. From the different things we'd been talking about, him and Honor were definitely good people. I just sat and stared at him while he talked. I was so in love with his dark brown skin, full long beard, and his dreads that he had up in a bun on top of his head, and baby, whatever cologne he was wearing, I for sure needed to know what it was.

"Why ya little creepy ass sitting there staring at me like that?" Thorne asked, ruining the moment.

"Sorry...I didn't mean anything about it. You just look and smell so good," I said, not meaning to say what I was thinking.

"You good, lil' mama, the way you sitting there staring at me turns me the fuck on. I'm trying to be patient with you because I know you don't know shit about being with a real nigga."

"Yo, you are so damn sure of yourself. What makes you think you gon' get that far with me?" I asked curious.

"You got a lot of damn mouth. I thought you were a little quiet weird thing at first green to everything. Can I ask you something without you feeling any type of way?"

"I can't promise you I won't feel some type of way, but you can ask me anything."

"Why were you letting Constance do all that stuff to you?"

"To be honest, I don't know. I just feel like she got me at a vulnerable time in my life. I felt like killing myself when my daddy died, Thorne, so at times I fought back, then others I just wished she had killed me. Losing both my parents has taken a toll on me. When I found out that Constance was poisoning me right then and there, I figured I needed to get my mind right, and don't be calling me weird. I'm different, but it's nothing wrong with that."

"You right, it's nothing wrong with that at all. Once I make you my girl, I'll show you everything you need to know."

"Is that so?" I asked with a raised brow.

Before Thorne got to say anything else, the waitress came out with our food. I didn't know what the rest of this night was going to bring, but what I did know was that this was the best I'd felt in weeks.

CHAPTER 22

Thorne

It had been a week and Rose and I had been inseparable; the shit was crazy if you ask me, but I was loving every bit of it. The streets were getting crazier, and I needed her; she was definitely my calm after the storm. Shit wasn't adding up about the shooting and I wasn't just feeling suspect about Pete and Dom now. I feel like Big Roy's ass is up to something too. Making me feel like I should have did what the big homie told me to do. I should have cut them a nice severance pay then got rid of them. I had a PI on Pete's ass so that's how I knew about him and strong face fucking around. For some reason that shit right there raised some red flags. I still had the PI working on shit, we were meeting up later so I could see what else his ass had found out for a nigga.

"What you in here doing?" Rose asked while entering my man cave, I had in my basement.

"Nothing just doing a little thinking and watching TV. What's up I thought you were sleep."

"I was but I woke up and you were gone."

Damn right I was gone her little ass keep rubbing her fat ass on me and I'm trying to be respectful. For a whole week we've been kissing and shit. I'm a grown ass man I'm sick of this making out shit. Thugs don't make out they be straight fucking. I don't wanna turn her off or upset her in any way, so I just be chilling.

The crazy part about all of this is Kreesha be calling me like crazy, but my mind is so caught up on Rose I ain't been checking for her at all. She even shot me text and said I heard you been spending ya time with a fat chick. I just looked at the text and laughed. Rose was not fat but thick as fuck baby girl was the shit in every way.

"My fault lil' mama I had some shit to handle. Are you hungry?"

"It's cool...I needed to get up. I'm going to spend the day with Honor today anyway. Speaking of Honor when are you going to talk to her Thorne."

I was getting sick of my mama and Rose keep asking me when I was going to talk to Honor. I would but not right now. I just wasn't ready. My monitor beeping bought us both out of our thoughts. I walked over to the bar where my monitor sat and saw my mama walking up with a mean mug on her face.

"I wonder what she wants this early in the morning."

"You didn't know she was coming?" Rose asked.

"No...she didn't call me last night or this morning."

"Oh ok...well I'll go answer the door for her. I was on my way to the kitchen anyway to see what you got to cook."

"Oh, shit you about to cook. Are we gone be straight afterwards or do I have to warn my mama now?"

"Boy shut up." Rose giggled. From the look that was on my mama's face I knew she was coming in here on one. I didn't know what her problem was, but I had enough shit going on. I didn't need her in here getting on my damn nerves today.

"So, you gone continue to act like the world revolves around your ass. I don't like this shit at all and you need to fix it. You got shit going on out here in these streets and you know damn well I don't trust nobody the only one I trusted is dead and then the other you not talking to him on some bullshit. Now I wasn't happy about Cace and Honor, but she's grown now Thorne. We raised her right she can handle herself. I'ma need you to get your shit together, and another thing if you don't mean Rose no good leave her the fuck alone. She's a good girl Thorne and she doesn't need no more bad luck in her life. Your older then her and I could tell she's not use to a man like you. Just like you don't know what it is to be with a damaged woman. A lot comes with her you just have to be gentle and love her the way she needs to be loved." My mama said all in one breath.

"Well damn mama...can I talk? You came right over here and read my black ass. I hear everything you're saying and I guess I need to fix it. And as far as Rose I really like her mama. I don't know what it is, but it's making me wanna help her, love her and treat her like the Queen she is."

"I hear you son and always remember a Thorne must protect his Rose no matter the situation. That's a little quote I heard a while back. Wow it's such a coincidence how you're falling for a woman name Rose. It so damn cute." My mama smiled. I couldn't do shit but laugh.

"Come on let's go see what Rose is doing. She said she was cooking breakfast." I said to my mama while we both headed up the steps. The sound of my monitor beeping again had me puzzled, because my immediate family were the only ones that knew where my crib was.

"Oh, Rose I hope you making a big breakfast because I told Cace and Honor to join us." I mean mugged my mama as I headed to open the door.

"I'll pull some more stuff out. It shouldn't be a problem." I walked over to the door and pulled it opened. I looked at Honor and she rolled her eyes. While Cace and I just mean mugged each other. I moved to the side and let them both in. Honor looked like she was in pain just had her arm in a sling and all bandaged up. I just looked at her and shook my head. Her little ass should have been home relaxing.

"Look all this quiet shit is getting out of control for no reason. Honor and I are together and I'm not interested in doing her wrong. I love her with all my heart regardless if you believe me or not. You can stay mad at me forever if you want, but when it comes to work and this street shit. I'm still here for you. This shit is my job too. So, we should be out here handling shit instead of being mad at each other for some shit that you can't change." Cace said.

"I'm still pissed with the both of you, because all you had to do was come to me. Yeah at first, I would have probably laughed at ya ass Cace. But nine times out of ten I would have been all for it. Yeah Honor is young, but you a good dude and I trust you with my life. So, of course I trust that you'll be good to her and protect her. As long as that's how this is going to be, I'm alright with y'all being together." I assured them both.

"Auntie must have come over here and chewed you a new ass hole." Honor giggled.

"Man, she came over here and set me straight about y'all and Rose too, she told me I better not hurt her."

"Welp...you better listen because if you do I'ma help auntie jump you."

"Baby can you go ahead in the kitchen with Rose. Let me talk to Thorne alone for a second."

"Alright...love you big head." Honor said when she walked off. Cace looked at her and smile then he winked at her.

"So, since you been booed up and not fucking with ya boy. I've been on the lookout, and some shit ain't been right. Big Roy, Pete, and Dom been moving funny as hell lately. It's like after Roy had that baby, he's been lazy with work. So, basically Wiley been covering for him and taking over the trap. Before you go try to kill Wiley let him be. He's been bringing good money in at that trap. I mean more money than when Roy was running it. Plus, we made need him to flip on his boy."

"What if he doesn't wanna flip on his boy?"

"Wiley all about money if the price is right. I'm sure he'll be down. Plus, we have gotten closer to Wiley and I've noticed he has strayed away from Roy lately. I asked him why and he said because he don't like the old heads and that's who Roy been fucking with."

"Yeah...I was just thinking about Pete, Dom, and Roy earlier. I've had a PI on Pete for weeks and why that nigga fucking Rose step mama ugly ass."

"You fucking lying?" Cace yelled out.

"Nope...and the way him and Dom been acting I wouldn't be surprised if they not the ones that offed Russ. I haven't reacted on it yet because I wanna get all my facts situated. I even got the PI digging shit up about Constance ugly ass. I'm meeting up with him later. You can roll out with me if you don't mind."

"Nah...I'm down. I also got Wiley looking up shit for me. So, we can go hit him up after that. What else you got in mind once we do all this. Let's just here everything out then we can react on it. Oh yeah and I need Wiley later don't he know Razor sick ass personally?"

"Razor that run the whore house out North?"

"Yup...when Rose was on the streets those two nights a girl name Meagan helped her and made sure she survived. Well that night in the park Razor was doing a recruit night and Meagan sacrificed herself, so he wouldn't see Rose. I promised Rose I was going to save her. I had forgotten about it until she asked me about it again last night."

"Oh, ok cool...don't know young girl need to be with Razor. I'm glad he didn't get his hands-on Rose because he would be dead as hell right now."

"Rose is beautiful and curvy in all the right places Razor would have hit the jack pot with her little young ass."

"Yeah you right. I'm glad he didn't get her. So, talk to me how you feeling about her?"

"A feeling I can't fucking describe. At first, I was second guessing myself because of her age, but I found myself thinking about her day in and out after that first kiss."

"Say what now...What kiss?"

"Long story that can be for another day. Let's go see if they done cooking a nigga is starving."

"Yeah she changing ya ass already. Nobody ever sat at your table for breakfast, lunch, or dinner. Now we going to be doing family shit, I guess." Cace chuckled and we both made our way into the dining room where Rose was now bring the food over to the table.

CHAPTER 23

Constance

I had been pacing the floor for days. Nothing about the original plan I set was going right. By now, I was supposed to be running my husband's empire with Dom's help. Yeah, y'all heard right, Dom. See, Pete wasn't strong enough. If he would have been listening from the beginning, he would have made sure Thorne's ass was gone.

"Mama...why you in here pacing the floor and talking to yourself? Are you OK?"

"Essence, leave me the hell alone. When you see me alone, don't fucking bother me unless you wanna get the shit beat out of you!" I snapped.

After I said what I said, Essence ran out of my room so fast. I was trying hard to keep my anger in, but lately, I had been snapping at my girls for everything. I could tell it was starting to bother them. When Russ was living and I would go through my episodes, he wouldn't let me as much as yell at my kids. So, they had it fucking lucky because when I was younger, I got it coming from both ways. My daddy would climb in my bed every chance he got and his simple ass wife would beat the shit out of me. My mama didn't want me anymore due to my daddy falling for another woman. Maritza and Clyde Boyd were my worst nightmares and if I ever found my mama today, I would kill the bitch for leaving me with them sick ass people.

"Mama...what's wrong with Essence?" Eboni asked, bringing me out of my thoughts.

"You know your sister is a little sensitive; she just got mad because I told her to leave me the hell alone," I assured Eboni. Essence was my weak link, and I knew if she ever got away from me, she would never come back. Russ would always holler at me for not letting them go away for college, but I wasn't letting my babies go anywhere; they were truly the only people that ever loved me.

"OK...well let me go talk to her. Are you sure you're good, Mama? You have been off a lot lately. Do you miss Russ?" Eboni asked.

"I'm good, baby, I promise you I am. Of course, I miss Russ, but you know the type of person he was. He would never want us down and out. You know he always talked to us about if he were to ever leave this world."

"Yes, I remember that, Mama. I miss him so much; he was really a good dude."

"I know he was, I miss him too. Now go ahead out, I need to get in the shower and take me a nap. Tell your sister I said sorry, I didn't mean to hurt her feelings."

"Alright...I will, Mama. Now get you some rest. I love you," Eboni said while kissing me on my cheek.

When Eboni left out, I made my way to the shower so I could wash this long day away. After I was satisfied with my shower, I got out, dried off, and slipped on my silk robe and laid across my bed in deep thought. The sound of my cellular phone going off brought me out of my thoughts.

Pete: Bring your ass out here to talk to me.

Me: Not right now, Pete. You know not to come to my house unannounced. My girls are here.

Pete: If you don't want me banging on the door and waking your girls up, you better meet me outside like I said.

Me: I can't stand ya ass.

Pete: You got five fucking minutes.

Not wanting him to wake the girls up, I jumped up off the bed and threw some tights, a t-shirt, and my flurry slippers then made my way out the door. Eboni was in the damn living room knocked out with the damn TV on, I would wake her up when I came back in. When I got out front, Pete was sitting on the hood of his car waiting for me. I was wondering what the fuck he wanted that couldn't wait till the morning.

"What could you had possibly wanted that you couldn't wait to discuss tomorrow?"

"I've been calling your fucking ass for almost a week now. Do you know anything about that shooting at the club? Thorne's cousin, Honor, got hit in the shoulder."

"What makes you think I had something to do with that shit?"

"Because I know you, sweetheart. Now don't fucking lie to me. Did you order that hit?"

"What if I did, Pete? What the fuck is you going to do about it? To be honest, this shit has nothing to do with me and you. So, just mind ya business and leave it the fuck alone!" I snapped.

"Connie...I keep telling you to stop talking to me like you don't got no fucking since. When I start knocking you upside your damn head, you gon' act like you know." I couldn't do shit but laugh. I wish his ass would try and hit me. I would kill his ass quick, fast, and in a hurry.

After laughing hysterically, I spread his legs apart and walked between them; making sure to get all up in his space. Then I grabbed the back of his head and pulled it to me and brought our lips together. I kissed him hard and rough, then I took my tongue and ran it from his lips to his cheek. Then I whispered in his ear, "Pete, don't you ever in your life threaten to hit me. The day that shit happens will be the day you fucking leave this earth. I mean it too--I put that on both my babies. Now if we finished out here, I would love to take my ass back to bed. I need to get my beauty rest for in the morning," I said sarcastically while sashaying my way back into my house. I could feel him looking at me, so I figured I would turn around and wink at him. Why did I do that? Pete ran up on me from behind and grabbed me by my neck and pulled me on the side of the house. He then pushed the front of me against the wall.

"What the fuck you doin', Pete?" I laughed.

"I'm doing what you want me to do," he said while forcefully pulling my tights down, then sliding his free hand around the front to play with my clit a little causing the flood gates to open. I leaned my head back on his shoulder while he entered me nice and slow.

"Fuck...Pete...just like that," I cooed while he drilled in and out of me in a fast motion causing my juices to run out of me and down my legs. The way he was moving, I knew he was soon about to reach his climax. The type of nigga Pete was, he always wanted me to get my nut first. So, he pulled out of me and got down on his knees then licked from front to back. The shit drove me wild and caused my body to shake vigorously. Once he felt me shaking all crazy, he hurried and held me up. Then in record breaking time, he slid right back in me giving me long, fast, deep, strokes. Pete pumped in and out of me until we both came long and hard. I leaned back on him while I panted.

Pete pushed me off of him causing me to hit the wall. I didn't know what his problem was, but it was definitely time for him to go.

"What the fuck is your problem? You gon' fuck me outside then treat me like a hoe?"

"Bitch...I ain't treatin' you no way. You been a hoe. When were you going to tell me that you were fucking Dom too? What you up to, Connie? You trying to tear friends apart? I'm already hip to your shit. You blinded me at first, but I'm good now. Ya pussy good, but not that fucking good to keep dealing with your crazy antics. Now I see what Russ meant by you's a special kind of crazy. I always thought he was just joking the way y'all used to laugh about it, but I wish he would have forewarned me. The crazy bitches always got the good pussy," Pete said while walking away.

"Fuck you...nigga, with your weak ass. Dom has always been a stronger man than you. Go ahead and take your bitch ass home and cry about it!" I yelled while throwing something at his car while I watched him pull off. I stormed off into the house and walked right into Essence with tears in her eyes.

"So, you've been sleeping with Pete, Mama? How long were you cheating on Russ? Is this something y'all had going on for years? Then you fucking him outside on the side of the house right under my window. Mama, what has gotten into you?" Essence snapped.

Forgetting that she was my child and I birthed her, I hauled off and punched her two times causing her to hit the floor. I then delivered two kicks to her side. Then I climbed on top of her and continued to deliver hit after hit.

"Mama, what the fuck are you doing?" Eboni screamed while pulling me off of her sister.

"You little bitches have no idea what I went through growing up. If you did, you would think twice about how you talk to me. Get her the fuck up and go to bed, NOW!" I yelled at Eboni.

I made my way into my bedroom and sat on my bed while shaking. I'd hollered at my kids, hit them, but it had never been this bad like they were chicks on the streets. I knew what I needed to do; it had been a minute since I had shown my face over that way, but Catherine Taylor needed to see me first thing in the morning. She was my therapist, and when I started dealing with Russ, I stopped going to see her because I felt like everything was going so good. I didn't know where it all went wrong at, but shit was definitely getting chaotic in my world.

CHAPTER 24

Rose

I was getting kind of over the point that I didn't know what happened to my banking information, so Thorne advised me to meet up with the lawyer alone. Thorne had been texting and calling him like crazy, but he hadn't been responding. Since he wasn't answering us, we decided to do a pop up on his ass. Now we were sitting outside his office waiting for him to pull up.

"Look at this nigga," Thorne said bringing me out of my thoughts. I looked up, and Mr. Shultz was getting out the car, looking over his shoulders like he was frightened.

"Why he lookin' like he scared to death?" I asked curious.

"I don't know, but let's get out and ask," Thorne said while jumping out of the car. When I got out of the car and when Mr. Shultz saw us it was like he had just seen a ghost.

"Hello, Mr. Williams...how are you? What brings you this way?"

Thorne practically choked him up by his neck and pulled him towards the door of the office.

"Me, you, and my girl got some shit to talk about. For some reason you haven't been responding to us, and to me, that makes me think some foul shit is going on, so I figured I would just pop up on ya Steve

Urkel looking ass today. Now let's go in so we all can have a seat."

"I'm sorry, Mr. Williams, I wasn't expecting to ever see you again."

"Hmm...you hear that, babe? He wasn't expecting to see me again. Why not, Mr. Shultz? Who assured you that you would never see me again? See, I knew I had some shit to discuss with you," Thorne said while now pulling the lawyer by his tie. It was so funny, but I didn't wanna laugh. Thorne had a feeling that the lawyer and Constance had something going on, so that was another reason why he pushed the issue for me to come see him. Thank God we were now in the office; I thought Thorne was going to choke the man to death.

"Ok, Mr. Shultz...I'm Rose, Russel Sanchez's daughter. For some reason, I think you know why I'm here," I said while sitting down in a chair across from him. While Thorne was standing right next to him in case he gets out of line. Mr. Shultz's eyes widened at the sound of my name.

"I have all the information of everything that is rightfully yours. I never reached out because Constance and her goons threatened to kill me and my whole family. I never told her what I had. I just agreed that I wouldn't reach out to you. I was just waiting until you showed up, even though she assured me that you were never going to show up and that Mr. Williams had no reason to come back. I just put my mind at ease, but when Mr. Williams started reaching out to me, I sent my family away for a little while. Constance is a very dangerous woman. Like she has real life mental issues, and I think she needs to be put away. This is why I'm sure your daddy came to me months before he was killed and changed his whole will."

"So, let me get this straight, you didn't tell her anything, but she still didn't kill you?" Thorne asked.

"I didn't lie to her about anything, I just didn't tell her anything. See, when Russ came to me and changed the will, he didn't tell anyone, and he left me complete instructions of how to do things. One of my instructions were to never tell her anything about what was given to Rose. He asked me to just play like he left everything to you. He figured she would have to work hard to get rid of you, but it would be easy to get rid of Rose, so to keep from putting his daughter in danger he told me to make it look good, so that's what I did. Now when he came to me, I had a feeling something was weighing on his heart heavy, but he never said anything. It was like he knew his time on earth was coming to an end," Mr. Shultz stressed.

"Wow...this is all crazy. Did he leave the information for my account with you?" I asked.

"Yes...he told me everything about what to do with the money your mama left you. It's all in an account ready for you to do whatever you want with it. Can I please get up and go over to my safe, to take all of the paperwork out so we can go over it together? You also have a couple of deeds."

"Yes...you go 'head and get whatever you need," Thorne demanded. Mr. Shultz walked back over with a box and a couple of folders.

"OK, Ms. Rose...for starters, you are a very rich young lady. I know that will not bring your parents back, but they made sure you were straight for the rest of your life. Not only do you have businesses, you own both of your parents' homes. The one your mama had in Georgia, the one Constance and her girls live in now, and your daddy had another home in Atlanta county which is only about an hour away. You could either live in it, sell it, or rent it out. It's yours to do whatever you want. He also made you and Mr. Williams here co-owners of both the bar and grills he was about to open. You are also the owner of his midnight blue Mustang, black Charger, and burgundy Benz truck."

"You good, babe?" Thorne asked. I was starting to feel a little flushed, so I knew my face was red. I knew my daddy was the man, but I never expected him to leave me all of this stuff. Money yeah, but houses, cars, and businesses? Like wow...I was nineteen and had more shit than I knew what to do with it.

"Yes...I'm good, I just don't know how to take all of this."

"Oh...yeah, and he wanted me to tell you and Mr. Williams this. He wanted you both to know this together because he knew Thorne could help you find out if it was true." Now Thorne and I were both looking at Mr. Shultz waiting to see what the fuck he was talking about.

"Come on, Shultz, spit that shit out. I need to know what the fuck is going on!" Thorne snapped because he was taking too damn long.

"Well, he thinks your mama was murdered. He doesn't know if Constance did it herself, but he would bet money that she had something to do with it."

"Wait, what? That's not possible, my mama had a heart attack. She's always had heart problems," I cried out. I felt my eyes getting watery, and it was to the point I didn't wanna hear any more. Thorne ran over to me and pulled me in for a hug. He held me while I cried on his shirt.

"Shultz, is there anything else I need to know?" Thorne asked.

"Yes...there's more, but if she can't take it, we can resume tomorrow."

"No...I know this much, so tell me the rest."

"As you know, your father was murdered. He gave me a name and an address for you to go see some man. I believe its Constance dad. He said he will tell you everything you need to know about Constance's crazy ass."

"You know what has me so confused about all of this? Russ was a powerful guy. How could he let himself get taken out?"

"This was above him, trust me. This is why you have to go see Constance dad. After you hear what he has to tell you, you should have a better understanding as to why things went the way they went. Russ told me to assure you both after all of this is said and done. You two shouldn't have no problems with living comfortably. Thorne, you have to remove all the weak links from your organization, and to his baby, Rose, you have to just stay on top of the world and continue to reach for the stars."

"Alright, Mr. Shultz, thanks so much for all you've done for us today. I'll make sure Constance gets what's coming to her, but go ahead with your family, and when I get all this taken care of, I'll give you a call giving you the OK to come back to town," Thorne assured him.

I was so in my feelings, all I wanted to do was head home and get in the bed while I cried on Thorne's chest.

CHAPTER 25

Thorne

Rose hadn't stopped crying yet. That bitch Constance had started some shit, that I was sure going to finish. I didn't know how or when, but for sure she needed to be counting her fucking days. The part when Shultz said this shit was above Russ had me so clueless. If that was the case why didn't he tell me maybe I could have helped. Ever since I talked to Shultz, I just keep saying to myself why didn't he ask me for help.

"Listen little mama I'm going to help you get down to the bottom of this if it's the last thing I do. I promise I'ma make everything right for you." I assured her as I pulled her in for a hug and held her while she cried. We had finally got back in the house after the long morning we had. I was going to call Cace so we could make that trip later to see Constance pops.

"I know you will Thorne. This all is just too much for me. How could someone be so hateful?"

"I don't know but go ahead and lay down for a little while I make a couple of phone calls." I said while kissing Rose on her forehead. After she made her way into the bedroom. I pulled out my phone to call Cace.

"Yo, bro what's good with you? Did you find out anything useful?"

"Man, I found out so much but I can't tell you about it until we get together later. I'ma hit you up after I take a nap."

"Ok...see you later bro. Text me when you wake up.

The feeling of the bed moving caused Rose to jump up. I wasn't trying to disturb her I just wanted to climb in the bed and hold her. I hated seeing her hurting, the shit made me ready to off everybody.

"I'm sorry ma I didn't mean to startle you. I just wanted to climb in the bed to hold you."

"I'm sorry I've been such a cry baby all day today Thorne. This is all just too much for me. Both my parents are dead and I still can't catch a fucking break. When will life get better for me Thorne." Rose asked while scooting over closer to me and climbing in my lap. I looked into her sad eyes then kissed her lips. I knew deep down inside that she was dealing with some deep shit. I could never imagine losing my mama, but Rose had loss both her parents. I knew shit was deep for her.

"Baby you don't have to apologize. When I started dealing with you, I knew exactly what came along with it. I wanted you so it's my job to help you get through all of this."

I ran my hand down Rose's smooth face. Then pulled her in for another kiss. It was something about me making her feel good that came to mind. Right at this very moment I wanted to take her mind off of all the bullshit that was going on in her head.

"How are you feeling about all of this. I'm sorry for never taking your feelings into consideration. I know you loved my daddy just as much as I did." Rose asked catching me off guard. I knew the sad look in my eyes answered her question. I knew we both were dealing with this heartache together, but I would never show it. I needed to be her strength and I was going to do just that. I couldn't help myself I leaned over and kissed her lips once again. Our tongues were now intertwine and dancing around in each other's mouth. I laid her down on the bed and climbed on top of her.

"Rose, can I take all your problems away for a little bit?" I asked seductively between kisses. Rose didn't speak but she nodded her head giving me the ok.

"Are you sure you want this lil' mama? If not, I'll wait until you're ready." I asked before I started. I started taking her clothes off. Once she was completely naked. I pulled my shirt over my head, then I started to kiss her all over her body. From her forehead ending up at her breast. When I made my way down to her breast, I noticed how she kept her arms crossed around her body like she was afraid to show it. I stopped kissing and stared right into her eyes for a minute.

"I don't want you to cover up. I wanna see every part of your beautiful body" I assured her.

After kissing and showing both her breast some much needed love. I eased my way down to her navel, making my way down to her pussy.

"What are you doing Thorne?" Rose asked looking kind of confused.

"I wanna taste your sweet spot. Just lay there and let me do me. I'm sure you'll enjoy every bit of it. I knew from the way Rose reacted when my tongue hit her clit that she never had this done. I grabbed both her ass cheeks and pulled that pussy deeper into my face. She was sweet and had a very fresh smell. I could tell she hadn't been touched in years, just like Honor had told me. I was glad to be that person to show her the real way for someone to make love to you. I locked down on her clit causing her to yell out in pleasure while climbing the walls. I began to move my tongue in and out of her in a fast motion causing her legs to jerk. Rose began to moan out in pleasure while I brought her body to her first orgasm.

"You ok beautiful? I asked while looking deep into Rose's eyes. Rose nodded her head letting me know that she was good.

"You ready for this dick baby?" I asked.

"Yes...but please be gentle with me. The last time I did this it was about three years ago and the guy wasn't as big as you at all." Rose said in a scared tone.

"I got you ma, my attentions are to make you feel good and to take your mind away from reality for a little while." I played with Rose's clit for a little bit to get her juices started again. Then I moved my finger in and out of her opening to loosen it up a little. I then eased my erection into her warm, wet, tight tunnel. The way she tensed up at first, I knew it hurt just a little. But once I got in all the way after a couple of strokes, I felt her fucking me back from the bottom. So, I knew she was starting to enjoy me moving in and out of her. I explored Rose's body for the next couple of hours until we both drifted off to sleep.

****

"Nigga I thought we weren't going anywhere tonight. I was calling ya ass like crazy."

"I know my bad Rose and I were sleeping good. She had a rough day after we met up with Shultz."

"I'm sure she did after all the shit you just told me. I wanna go kill that bitch Constance myself." Cace stressed.

After the session Rose and I had we both went to sleep. Her ass was still knocked out when I left the house.

"Are you sure somebody lives in this dump, bro?" Cace asked bringing me out of my thoughts.

I looked up and we pulled up in front of an old dark house. It didn't look abandon it just looked like one of those big ass houses that be on scary movies. I parked the car a little down from the house. Then I pulled the address out of my pocket.

"Yup...that's the address that's on the paper. Come on let's get out and see what this shit is all about."

"You got ya burner?"

"Of course, I do. What about you?"

"Never leave home without my bitch."

Cace and I walked over to the house and up the steps locked and loaded just in case we were walking into some bullshit. I pulled my gun from the small of my back and began to knock on the door with the tip of it.

"Who the hell is it?" A loud groggy voice said from the other side of the door.

"My name is Thorne and I'm here to talk to you about Constance. Russ sent me."

The door opened and a tall thin man with Constance whole face opened the door. It was absolutely scary how much she favored him.

"Is she dead yet or is she locked away?" He asked while leaving the front door open and while he walked away. I assumed he was giving us the ok to walk in so that's what I did and Cace followed suit. When we walked all the way in it was henny and beer bottles everywhere. We knew for sure this man didn't miss a drink.

"Mr. Clyde Boyd...we received your information from Russel's lawyer. He wanted us to pay you a visit so you can tell us a little about your daughter. Did you talk to Russ at all before he died?" I asked. He kind of hesitated but then he shook his head yes.

"They were on to her and I had to do what I had to do." Clyde said.

Me and Cace looked at each other confused like hell. Like what was his crazy nigga talking about.

"Who was on to who?" I asked curious.

"Maritza's family was on to my baby."

"Listen mutha fucka we tired of you talking in riddles. We don't even know of these people that your fucking talking about."

"Maritza Almaraz was my wife. Me and her did terrible things to Constance while raising her. Which is why she's the monster she is today. I'm not proud of the man I was, but I needed help back then. Now that I know that I'm pissed off that I took the shit out on my daughter. Not only was I doing things to her I allowed my wife to beat the shit out of her every chance I got."

"Wait...is Maritza Almaraz apart of the Almaraz Cartel?" Cace asked causing me to look up at him.

"Yes...she was the only daughter."

"Well what happened to her?"

"At seventeen years old Constance got tired of Maritza putting her hands on her. So, while I was out of town, she started poisoning Maritza. One night she had put something in her food. Then set the house on fire. When I got back from my work trip. My wife was dead and my daughter had run away. I never looked for her because I was afraid of her telling the authorities what I did to her. One night about five months ago Russ came to see me, because he had noticed a change in Constance and she was taking it out on the girls. He said she wasn't actually hitting them but she was a little snappy and punishing them for crazy shit and not wanting them to go away to college. I then sat him down and told him about Constance's childhood and he beat the shit out of me. I was in the hospital for about a week when he got finished with me. So, I was so fucking pissed I went to the Cartel and told them he killed Maritza because I owed him money. When I got the phone call about him being dead, I knew what had happened."

"Let me get this straight you got him killed because he beat ya bitch ass up. When the one you should have been turning in is ya crazy ass daughter. How do you know what happened if your daughter ran away?

"When she got grown, she came back over here to show me how she was doing despite of how she grew up. We talked for hours and she confessed. Knowing that we fucked her life up I didn't say shit. I kept her secret and she kept mine."

"So ya perverted ass was fucking your daughter. That's probably why your wife was beating her because she was jealous. She couldn't compete with young in-house pussy. But her ass must have had issues too because why didn't she leave ya sick ass. Get the fuck up and show me where the fucking Cartel is?" I snapped while hitting Clyde across the head with my gun.

"Wooh...Thorne we can't just walk up in the Cartel. Are you crazy? That's what Shultz meant when he said this was above Russ. By the time he probably realized what was going on it was too late. I say we just kill this sick mutha fucka then make his daughter kill who ever offed Russ. So, that way we won't have shit to do with it."

Cace had a good point we didn't need no heat on us after we were done getting rid of Dom, Pete, and Constance we should be good. I looked at Clyde and pointed my gun at his temple.

"Do you have any last request old man?" I asked.

"Yes...can you tell my daughter I said I'm sorry I didn't mean to ruin her life." Clyde said right before I sent him to meet the maker.

"Come on bro...let's get the fuck out of here before someone calls the police." Cace said while heading for the front door.

"Ain't nobody calling the cops in this crazy ass looking neighborhood, but we do got shit to go plan out." Cace and I headed to the car jumped in and pulled off.

CHAPTER 26

Constance

My phone rung about five times before I decided to pick it up. I looked at the number, and it was the same number that called me at least five times today so I figured I would just go ahead and answer it.

"Hello, can I speak to Constance Boyd?"

"This is her; may I ask who's calling?"

"Hello ma'am...my name is Detective James, and I'm calling to inform you that your father was found dead this morning."

I didn't feel any type of way to be honest. I didn't even know why he would put me down as his next to kin. I wasn't going to go identify shit. This man sexually abused me for years. I could care less that he was dead or alive.

"How did he die?" I asked.

"A single shot to the head," the detective said.

"Good, I wish they would have shot him in his dick first to remind him that it wasn't supposed to be inside of little girls. Do me a favor and roll his ass in a wood box and throw him in the dirt. You could even burn him if you want. I don't give a damn, just don't call me the fuck again!" I yelled right before hanging the phone up.

"Mama...are you good?" Eboni asked.

"Yes...that was the cops telling me that your grandfather is dead."

"Oh wow...are you OK?"

"Yes...baby, I'm fine. That man was never good to me. That's why I never let y'all meet his sick ass." The sound of banging on my front door caused us both to jump. I walked to the front door with Eboni right behind me.

"Who is it?" I yelled

"It's Rose."

I couldn't believe this fat bitch had the nerve to come back to my fucking house after being gone for weeks. I opened the door, and she was standing there with Thorne. She had some type of glow to her, and she didn't look depressed with bags under her eyes. Not to mention she was laced in the finest shit, making me wonder where the fuck she got it from, but then again, she probably was fucking this damn boy.

"What do I owe the pleasure of this visit?"

"Bitch...it's almost eviction day." Thorne chuckled.

"I came to discuss some things with you and your daughters. Can I come in?"

Eboni looked at me, and I looked at her. I moved to the side and let them both in. I walked into the living room with them following behind. I sat on the couch and turned my attention to them.

"You have to be out of here by tomorrow night," Rose said.

"Wait, what the fuck are you talking about?"

"I found out everything about you down to your sick ass childhood. It all makes since now; your step mama kicked your ass, so you decided to kick mine. You cheated on my daddy with numerous men due to you being promiscuous all because of your father molesting you. Truth of the matter is, you need to be dead or locked away in a mental institution. I started to turn you in for poisoning me just like you did your step mama when you were a teenager, but we need you for something."

"Why would I do something for your sorry ass?"

"It's not a request, but first I need to know why you killed my mama. Pete told us everything, so you might as well enlighten us on what really went down. What made you snap the way you did? Were you mad because my daddy didn't leave ya cheatin' ass a thing?"

"You little bitch, ya daddy never loved me anyway. All he ever gave a fuck about was ya mama, so I figured if I deleted her from the equation, I wouldn't have to worry about him cheating on me.

Whap...Whap...Whap...Whap! Rose walked over to me and hit me across my face four good times. I was about to get up, but then Thorne pulled his gun out.

"Bitch, if you move, I'll blow your fucking head off right in front of your daughter." Thorne grimaced.

"My daddy did love my mama, but he loved ya crazy ass too. You know why he dead, he's dead because after he found out what ya daddy did to you, he beat the shit out of him, and ya bitch ass daddy went and told the cartel that it was my daddy that killed Maritza Almaraz, but it was you," Rose stressed.

I sat there with my mouth wide open because I didn't even know that's why Russ was dead. My daddy had a way of ruining my fucking life. He struck once again.

"Now as I was saying, you have till tomorrow to get the fuck out of my house. Eboni and Essence are welcome to stay until they find somewhere else to go, but you are out of here. We're even going to pick you up and take you where you need to go. Yeah, because all the cars were left to me too including the burgundy

BMW that you've been pushing around. Oh, and don't try to leave because if you do, we will find you. Now, where is Essence?"

"She's in her room resting," I assured her.

"That's funny because Essence spends most of her time down here when she's home. Baby, I'm going upstairs to check on her."

"OK...I'll be down here waiting on you when you get back, and don't take too long. I may have to kill one of these bitches if they talk shit."

"Let me find out you rescued her from here so you could fuck her," I sassed.

"Bitch, I rescued her because she was being mistreated, and now, I'm here to help her have a good life. After all the fucking chaos you caused you better be glad, she has a good heart after everything you did to her. Because my suggestion was to throw you and all your shit out on the front lawn then shoot you right in between the eyes. Don't get mad because Rose is loved, you crazy ass bitch!" Thorne barked while knocking me upside my head.

"Thorne, what the hell did you do to her?" Rose asked while walking down the steps with Essence behind her.

"Nothing...I told you I was going to fuck this bitch up if she talks shit, and guess what, she was talking shit. Are you ready to go? I'm sick of being here. Plus, we have to meet up with Wiley, he has Meagan."

"Alright cool, but Essence is coming with us. Constance has been hitting on her, and now she's scared to come out of the room. Eboni, would you like to come with us too?" Rose asked.

"Nah...I'm good right here with my mama. Essence, I can't believe you're leaving with these people and they're doing this to our mama," Eboni said while rolling her eyes.

"The only reason you still love her like that is because you don't get beat on. You've always been the strongest daughter, so since you weren't weak, she didn't fuck with you. See, me and Rose was weak in her eyes which is why she used us for punching bags. I hope you take Rose up on her offer and stay in this house until you find something else. Because being around her could cost you your life. You see what she did to Rose's mama," Essence said.

"So, I brought you into this world, and this is how you do me? It's cool though because ya weak ass ain't gon' last in this cold, cold world. Rose is not going to be around all the time to save you!" I yelled while they walked right out of the door. All of this was crazy, but the even crazier part was I never thought my own flesh and blood would walk out on me.

CHAPTER 27

Rose

I had Thorne take Meagan and Essence to my house in Atlanta County until I had the house that Constance was in cleaned and renovated. Truth was, I was going to give the house to Eboni and Essence. I just needed Constance out of the way. Today I was going to the warehouse with Thorne, Wiley, and Cace. They had all of them chained up to chairs. We knew the bulk of the story, but Thorne needed to know everything before he sent Dom and Pete on their way. We already knew what we were doing with Constance, and we were using Eboni as collateral. See, Constance loved Eboni more than anything in the world, and I believed that was because of her being her mother's child. See, I actually could see that Eboni was going to end up like her mama. I hope to God that she didn't have any kids. Some people were just not meant to be mothers.

"You ready, baby?" Thorne asked me, bringing me out of my thoughts.

"Yeah...I'm so ready to get this over with so we can get back to living a normal life."

"OK...now, are you sure? I know you're not used to this type of shit, and I could handle it all alone if need be. I don't want you having nightmares or anything."

"Thorne...I'll be fine. I've been living a nightmare for the past seven months. If this shit right here is about to make them stop, then I'm all for it."

"Alright...just was double checking, that's all. I never want you in an uncomfortable situation. I'm here to make everything better for you, so if you're ever feeling any type of way about anything, please tell me, and I'll fix it, and that goes for everything, Rose. If you ever feel like the street life is in the way of our relationship, let me know, and I'll leave it all alone for you. I'm already in the process of cleaning some of this money, and I have a couple people in line to take over when I'm ready to have a family of my own."

"Wow...that's good to hear that you have future plans and that the streets are not something that you plan do until you're old and gray. I think I have an idea, and it just came to my head."

"What is it? Run it by me."

"I was thinking about fixing that house up that Constance was in and make a home for homeless young girls. Like a safe house or something like that. We give room and board, job search classes, food, counseling, and help them find jobs and homes. We can call it *"The Cinderella House."* When I was on the streets those two nights, there were so many young women out there, Thorne, it was horrible. I just want them to have somewhere safe to go to. I want them to be safe from all the Razor's that are in the world. Speaking of Razor, what did y'all do to him?"

"Nothing, we had to pay him for Meagan, that's all, and we made him sign papers that he would never come for her again. If he does, we kill him."

"Oh, I thought y'all would have killed him."

"Nah...we know Razor from the hood. Yeah, he may be doing shit that we don't approve of, but that's still a part of the street code. Now if he touches family, then he's as good as dead."

I nodded my head at Thorne letting him know that I understood. My daddy did his job keeping me away from the streets, but I wasn't sure that was the right decision. Just because your parents were into to it didn't mean you had to, but I felt like if I knew, I wouldn't be so green to everything.

"Enough about all that shit, let's get back on your idea. That shit is a dope ass idea, ma. We could sit down when you ready and figure out how you wanna go about everything. You already know I'm down to help you with whatever."

I loved Thorne already but was scared to tell him. I was scared that he would think it was too fast to be using the love word. Plus, I was young as shit; did I even know what love was? This was something that I had been pondering on for the past couple of days. Thorne's phone started to ring. He looked down at it then hit ignore. I thought it was kind of suspicious being as though he usually answered it, but I decided to leave it alone.

"OK, good...I can't wait until we get it started. I'm excited about this."

"Don't worry, we gon' get it all figured out, baby girl," Thorne assured.

A half hour later, we were now pulling up to the warehouse. It was crazy how all the men would be in attendance, but I would be the only woman. Honor told me that Cace wouldn't let her, and I didn't know if Wiley had a chick he dealt with or not. I didn't have to be here, but Thorne always gave me an option. He told me if something happened to him, I would be next in charge to run the empire. I looked at him like he was crazy, but he assured me that Cace and Wiley would make sure I was good.

"Come on, baby, let's go." Thorne bought me out of my thoughts when he opened the car door for me.

"Y'all took long as shit. I was getting sick of standing out here." Wiley chuckled.

"Nigga...you could have sat ya fat ass on top of your car." Thorne laughed.

"Nigga...fuck you," Wiley said while dapping Thorne up.

"Hey, sis!" Cace said while pulling me in for a hug.

"What's up, y'all?" After we all said our hellos, we entered the warehouse. The smell was awful, it almost made me gag. It reeked of piss and horrible body odor. I didn't know how long they'd been in here, but I knew it had to be a couple days. Cace walked over to a table that sat right outside the door of the room where I assumed, they all were being held.

"Here sis, here goes a mask for you." He gave me a mask to put over my face. It had a clean scent to it which I was happy about because I wasn't sure if I would have been able to go in the room with it stinking like that. They all put a mask on, then we all entered the room.

"Well fellas...how the fuck have y'all been doing in here?"

"What the fuck is going on here?" Dom asked.

"You tell me what the fuck is going on. Word on the street is that y'all needed to get rid of me, so tell me who was trying to get rid of me. Tell me who's idea it was?"

"It was all her idea! Pete yelled out.

The crazy part about all of this, I was shocked about Pete even being involved in this. My mama always felt some type of way about Dom, but she loved Pete.

"How I knew you were going to be the first person to speak up. So, it looks like you'll be getting the first hit."

"I can't stand a snitch, bro; can I kill his mutha fucking ass now?" Wiley asked.

"No...not yet. I'm still trying to see who the fuck thought they were big and bad enough to kill me, so let me just get started on all the bullshit I've been hearing about y'all. First of all, you both got played. Her ass was trying to get on the empire but was going to make you two go against each other and end up killing one another, but what she failed to realize was that she still wouldn't have anything to do with the empire. As long as Rose is still alive, no matter if she wants it or not, it's still hers in my absence. You ready to talk, baby?" Thorne asked.

"I just wanna know, why? Why would you all do all of this as much as my daddy did for all of you? Constance, my daddy took ya bat shit crazy ass in and helped you raise your girls and gave you the world. Pete, you've been around since I was born. My daddy put ya broke ass on, and you been living good ever since. Dom, I never understood how he even trusted you. You look like you can't be trusted, so if my daddy wouldn't have gotten killed by the cartel, would y'all have taken him out?" I asked, and no one responded. Thorne walked up on Pete and pulled his gun from the small of his back and hit Pete right in the lips, and blood flew out of his mouth.

"I know y'all mutha fuckas hear my girl talking to y'all."

"Well, you already know why I was turning on your father. He should have thought about the shit he was doing to me." I reached for Thorne's gun, and he looked at me like I was crazy.

"Gimme your gun, babe," I said in a serious tone, and he looked at me again with a crazy face. The look I gave him, he didn't ask any questions, he just handed it over with no problem. I took the butt of the gun and hit Constance right upside the head. I didn't wanna get her in the face because I knew she needed to be presentable. The blood started running down her head, and she screamed.

"You fucking stupid bitch, why would you do that?"

"Maybe it'll knock some sense in your fucking head. I told you my daddy loved you. He's dead for feeling sorry for your stupid ass and got caught up. If he didn't care about you, he would have put ya bat shit crazy ass out on the curb, but no, he cared about you and tried to defend you!" I screamed. I was shocked because my ass wasn't crying. My adrenaline was going, and believe it or not, I wanted to shoot her ass, but Thorne grabbed the gun from my hand.

"You OK...baby?" Thorne asked looking concerned.

"Yeah...I'm good, I'm just ready for that bitch to die. Kill them assholes and let's hurry up and get her on the job so her time can be up."

"I keep telling y'all I ain't doin' shit for y'all."

"Oh, but you will. If not, Eboni is as good as gone. We have her locked up in one of the warehouse rooms right now. Wiley, show her your phone."

When Thorne went to pick Constance up from the house, I told him to grab Eboni because I felt like she didn't care about anybody but Eboni, and the way her eyes lit up, I knew we had her right where we needed her at.

"Baby, we can go as soon as I find out who was the mastermind behind this bullshit they had going on."

I was really ready to go, and we already knew what happened because what Pete didn't already tell us Roy had told Thorne and Cace. So, I didn't know what exactly Thorne was trying to prove. All this started because Constance got mad when she found out my daddy was grooming Thorne to take over in his absence. Constance did all this bullshit for no reason. Yeah, this bitch needed some meds. Cace walked over to Dom and punched him right in the mouth.

"You assholes need to start fucking talking."

"You know what, I got something for they asses since nobody wants to talk," Wiley said while pulling his knife out of his pocket. "How about I cut Pete's fucking tongue out?"

"Come on man, please, I already told you who's idea it was," Pete cried out. Wiley walked over to him and demanded that he stick his tongue out, but Pete didn't; instead, he just started telling us everything that we already knew. Once Pete was finished, Wiley pulled his gun out and shot him right in the side of his head. Then Thorne walked up on Dom and shot him right in the forehead.

"OK baby, we can go now. What you wanna do with Constance?"

"Leave that bitch in here until tomorrow; we can't chance her getting the fuck away."

"OK cool...Wiley, call the clean up to come handle these bodies. Tell them don't touch her. If they do, they'll have to answer to me," Thorne retorted.

We all headed out the warehouse like we didn't have a care in the world. Today was definitely different for me, and I didn't feel bad about it at all. I couldn't wait to get rid of Constance's ass tomorrow. I guess the shit I'd been through the past couple of weeks had turned me into a cold-hearted person.

CHAPTER 28

Thorne

Rose and I had showered, and now she was sleeping. I had a couple of phone calls to make, but I didn't want to wake her, so I decided to go down in my man-cave. After I talked to Wiley to make sure they handled them bodies, I laid my phone on the bar so I could pour me a shot of Henny. I heard beeping from the monitor, and the shit caused me to grab my burner from behind the bar. I looked at the monitor, and I didn't believe what the fuck I just saw. Kreesha's ass was walking up my front steps. I hurried and ran up the steps and to the front door before she started banging. I opened the front door, and her ass had tears in her eyes. I also could smell the liquor from a distance.

"Kreesha, what the fuck are you doing here? How did you find out where I lived?"

"I've been fucking calling you for weeks, and you haven't been answering me, so I followed you from your mama's house. Why the fuck I didn't know about this house, Thorne? What about us? What happened to what we had? You just stop calling and everything. I heard you got a girl. Is this true?" Kreesha slurred her words.

"Come on, Kree ...you knew what type of relationship we had, so why the fuck you actin' all crazy now? You need to get the fuck from in front of my house before I beat ya ass!" I snapped while looking back at the door to make sure Rose didn't come down.

"I'm not going anywhere until you fucking answer me, Thorne."

"Kree, you already know what the fuck it is, so don't come the fuck over here with this bullshit."

"Don't tell me what the fuck to do, Thorne. What you gon' do, pull out ya gun and shoot me for not getting off your property? No...call ya bitch out here and tell her to make me leave. Where the fuck is she, Thorne?"

Thank God I didn't have any neighbors and my house sat by itself on a bunch of land. This bitch was getting on my fucking nerves with all this damn hollering. I kept looking at the door praying Rose wasn't standing there, but the last time I turned around, she was already standing there looking at me with a me mug.

"Thorne, get her the fuck away from here. I had a long day, and I'm trying to sleep. If I'm going to be having problems with chicks popping up, I can go stay at my own shit," Rose sassed, shocking the hell out of me.

I had enough of this bitch. I grabbed her by her arm and snatched her up and dragged her to her car. I pushed her into the car then I climbed in the passenger seat. I pulled my gun out and put it to her temple.

"Kree, you know the type of dude I am, and you already knew I was interested in someone because I told you. Why you think I haven't been coming around? We already had this discussion, so I don't even know why you even came over here with the bullshit, so now what you gon' do is leave from in front of my house and don't return. If you do, your mama will be buying a black dress to bury ya ass in. Do I make myself clear?" I asked while pushing the gun into the side of her head making sure she could feel it.

"I only came over here because I love you, Thorne."

"I get all that, ma, I really do, but I'm in love with somebody else, and the longer I'm out here talking to you, I'm being disrespectful, so take ya ass home before you won't never make it there again."

"So, this fast, you love her?" Kreesha asked.

"Yes...I do to the point I have no desire for anyone else."

"Alright, then Thorne...you don't have to ever worry about me anymore. Now get the fuck out of my car before I call the cops and tell them you beat me the fuck up."

"Yeah...OK, do that shit, and your mama will definitely be burying her baby girl." I jumped out of Kree's car, and she peeled off. I couldn't believe her crazy ass came over here on the bullshit. I never found out how she got my address, but it was cool though. If her ass showed up again, I was killing her.

I walked in my house and turned off all the lights then grabbed me a bottled water and made my way up the steps. I got to my room, and Rose was sound asleep. I walked all the way in the room and stripped out of my clothes. As soon as I climbed in the bed, Rose turned to look at me.

"You finally got your bitch to leave, I see," Rose sassed.

"Yeah...she finally left. I had to threaten to kill her in order for her to go. I know what you thinking, but I been told her about us. I also been left her alone since Honor's party. When I saw you, my mind was on you, so I had no intentions on dealing with her ever again. My mind was set to get you, and I did."

"Oh, really?" Rose said while straddling me. Then she leaned in and started nibbling on my ear.

"Mmm...what you doin' with ya little fresh ass?" I asked, enjoying what Rose was doing. It didn't take her no time to start showing her freaky side in the bedroom, and I loved every bit of it. Of course, it was some things I had to teach her which was fine. She could be my little freak.

"I'm trying to get you to put me back to sleep. Since ya little girlfriend woke me up," Rose cooed while whispering in my ear.

"Didn't I just give ya little ass some before you went to sleep? I see you comin' out of that little shell you were in, and I'm liking every bit of it."

"Yeah...you did, but I want more, and I want it now."

"Hmm...a little demanding, don't you think? It's cool though because I ain't got no problem with giving you exactly what you want."

I was going to give Rose exactly what she wanted. Hell, I didn't mind going another round myself. It was like whatever she had in between her legs was addictive as hell, and I needed to be inside of her a couple of times a day.

While Rose was kissing on my neck, I was sliding out of my boxer briefs unleashing the beast. Rose then slid down on my erection causing me to moan like a little bitch. Her having on no panties made it all so much easier. She moved up and down on my dick while I watched her eyes go back in her head. Rose was starting to get carried away moving all crazy on my dick causing me to grab her waste to slow her down.

"Slow down, ma, I ain't ready to cum just yet. Move that thing nice and slow for me just like I taught you, baby," I insisted while I slid her shirt over her head exposing her big breasts. I slipped one in my mouth while I pinched on the other nipple. The shit was driving her crazy and causing my nut to build up. I could feel her pussy muscles tighten up on my dick while she began to move in a fast motion again. I couldn't help myself; we were about to catch this nut together.

I started drilling in and out of her from the bottom meeting her stroke for stroke. My toes were curling, and she was biting down on her bottom lip.

"Fuck...Thorne, I'm ready to cum, baby? I'm ready to cum," she moaned out in pleasure.

"Shit, me too, baby girl...me too...let's do this shit together."

The minute them words left my mouth, we both were cummin' at the same time. She leaned over to kiss my forehead, and all I could do was chuckle.

"You givin' forehead kisses now, ma?" I asked.

"Yup...and what's wrong with that?"

"Nothing at all, it's just funny how a couple of weeks ago how shy you were, and now you my little freak." I chuckled while kissing Rose on the lips.

"Thorne...do you think everything is going to go as planned tomorrow?" Rose asked.

"I'm sure everything is going to go fine, baby. Just go ahead to sleep. Don't worry yourself about it. If the plan that's set doesn't work, then we will take another approach. Now take ya ass to sleep, I thought that's why I just gave you that bomb ass dick to put ya little ass to sleep? It definitely was bomb." Rose giggled then yawned.

I was going to make sure she never had to worry about Constance again even if I had to take her out myself. I vowed that I was going to make sure Rose was good, and that was exactly what I was going to do.

I kissed Rose on the top of her head, and we both drifted off to sleep.

CHAPTER 29

Constance

L ast night I was sitting in that cold warehouse sitting in my own bodily fluids. In between a couple of corpse until they came to remove the bodies. I couldn't do shit but cry for the entire night worried about my baby. Seeing that picture of her lying in a warehouse on a dirty mattress had me freaked out. I knew they meant business watching them kill Pete and Dom in front of me. I couldn't lose my daughter. I would rather them kill me instead, so I figured I had no other options but to do what the fuck they wanted me to do. They had figured out everything they needed to about Rickie Almaraz. How they found out what they knew was shocking to me, but they knew every Thursday night that he would be home alone for two hours the most. Another thing they knew was he liked his prostitutes. So, here I was getting dialed up by Thorne's little cousin Honor. After they got me dressed up, they had me talking to this sick fuck online. He did his shit through an agency called *Good Girls*. They had already had my profile ready and everything.

"So, what if I get here and he kills me first?" I asked.

"Then if you die first so does your daughter. You have simple instructions and there's no reason why you should fuck this up. The man is home alone."

"Understand what you're saying, but do y'all know that these are powerful people?"

"Your daddy didn't care how powerful they were when he went and lied on my daddy. Since they killed the king of my castle. I need the king of theirs dead." Rose snapped. I could tell she wasn't about to play with me today. Something about her was different and I didn't know what it was. All I know is that when she looks at me, I feel a cold stare. An hour later I was dressed and ready to go. Rickie Almaraz has sent a car for me and I was nervous as fuck.

Thorne and his little crew were a lot smarter than I thought. Now I was thinking about all the bullshit I done did and wished I never took it this far. Yeah, I finally came in terms with me needing meds to keep me sane. Forty-five minutes later I pulling up to a big ass mansion. I was so amazed about this home, but then I remembered that I had a job to do and I needed to stay focused. Once I exited the car the driver then walked me up to the front door where Mr. Almaraz was standing in the door watching me.

"Well hello beautiful," Mr. Almaraz said right before moving to the side so I could fit by him.

"You can go ahead and have a seat on the couch and I'll be right back." I watched him walk away with his silk robe on. Something was off about this asshole and I didn't like it. When he came back, he had drinks for me and him. He then sat next to me with a big ass smile on his face.

"So, you live in this big ass house alone," I asked trying to start a conversation.

"No...I have a whole family but they like to go out on Thursday's. I decided to stay in the house because I knew you were coming."

Rickie had thought that me and him were talking on the computer, but it was Rose and Honor socializing with him.

"Oh ok...you were ready for me all week, weren't you?" I asked seductively.

"Yes...I was, so what do you wanna do? I have a surprise for you whenever you're ready."

"No rush baby...get us some more to drink and let's sit and talk for a little while. So, tell me where is your wife?"

"My wife died shortly after our daughter did. I swear she died from a broken heart." Hearing him say that shit about his daughter kind of made my stomach turn. The to hear that his wife died from a broken heard sadden me once more.

"Oh, that's sad...will you ever marry again."

"Probably not, but I would love for us to head up to the bedroom. I only have a couple of hours before my family comes, but I also got some plans for us up in the room."

"Ok well lets go. You go ahead and follow the lead."

I had to get close to this fool ad inject this stuff that Thorne had gave me. Then shoot him right in his head. The gun they gave me had a silencer on it so no one could hear. I followed him up steps to the master suite. Once we made it into the room Ricki pushed me up against the wall and kissed me roughly while yanking on my hair. I guess the liquor was starting to take over his body because his ass was starting to put his hands everywhere.

"Take off all of your clothes and I have a surprise for you."

"Ohhh...I love surprises."

Once I was out of my clothes the only thing, I had on was a black panty and bra set. I looked around the room and everything seemed to be in the right spots. My stomach was down in my feet. I was so scared for my life, but I knew this was something I had to do to keep Eboni alive. I sat on the bed and waited for him to come back in here.

When Ricki came back in the room, he had two girls with him who look like they were about sixteen and seventeen. I looked at him like he done lost his damn mind.

"Here goes my surprise mami...we definitely are going to have tons of fun." Hearing how fascinated his trifling ass was had me furious. This explained why Maritza was deceased.

"I don't know what your intentions were, but I will not be getting in the bed with these little young girls. Are you fucking serious I snapped?"

"Yes, as serious as a heart attack. I paid you for the night already, so you're going to do what the fuck I hired you for. Or I will call your agency and have you fired."

"Well how about me and you get the party started." I said in a seductive tone walking over to him. Once I wrapped my arms around his neck. I placed a kiss right on his lips. While he was enjoying feeling all on me. I slid the syringe that I had hidden in my tights out and stuck his ass right in the neck.

"What the fuck did you just stick in me."

"Just a little something to spice up our night. Now go lay down and me and the girls are going to give you the show of your dreams." Ricki simple ass did what I told him to do, but by the time he laid down he was already out.

"Listen lady's go ahead to your room and put some clothes on. If you move fast you can leave with me." I assured the girls, and they both ran out of the room. I hurried over to Ricki grabbed a pillow and put it over his face. Then I pulled out the gun and pulled the trigger. After I made sure he was good and dead. I hurried and put my clothes back on then headed to one of the rooms to see where the girls were. Once I made it to their room I was confused because they both just chilling.

"Shit they didn't wanna go that was on they crazy asses. I hurried and made my way to the front door, but the minute I turned the knob a couple of men walked in. As soon as they saw me, they grabbed their guns.

"Who the fuck are you and what are you doing in here?"

"Listen...I could explain."

"Leo go check on papa." The first armed man said.

Welp I knew I wasn't getting out of this one for sure, but I did fulfill my job so that means Eboni will be fine. I couldn't call Thorne, but I knew the shit about Almaraz would be all over the news tomorrow,"

"He's gone Tony...he's gone Tony." No more words were spoken. Tony turned his gun to me.

"Who the fuck sent you?" Tony asked.

"Nobody sent me your father is a sick fuck and somebody needed to handle his ass. Y'all all chilling around in here when there are underage girls in here being used for all type of things."

"I don't know who this bitch is but you need to hurry up and kill her ass."

Pop...Pop...Pop...

Tony let off three rounds in me and I fell to the floor and everything went black. Now everything makes so much sense now. Maritza was crazy because she experienced abuse. I was an abuser because I experienced abuse. I just hope to God that history doesn't repeat itself with my girls.

EPILOGUE

Six months later
Rose

Life has finally started to look good for me. Out of everything my daddy left me the main thing that brings me joy is the center that I opened for homeless women. It has been open for about three months and the shit was doing amazing. Not only that Thorne has been a big help in all of this. Since he was ahead of the empire, he didn't have to dabble in the street stuff that often. He was the boss and he had workers to handle all that shit, so he was able to help me run my business. Instead of going away to school I started online courses. After all the shit I been through I wanted to be a Psychiatrist. Plus, I knew it would be good with me running the home. I had Meagan as a head counselor, Honor did hair and makeup on the weekends since she owned her own shop. Essence helped with the schooling part since she had started school for her teaching degree. I had hired her to work here until she finished school. Essence was doing good she just had some issues because we didn't have a clue where Eboni disappeared to. After the Cartel got rid of Constance her body was found in the Atlantic Ocean. It caused Eboni to leave that's how hurt she was. Constance was left a lot of money from her daddy, but since she died shortly after it was left to Eboni and Essence. But since they couldn't find Eboni and she wasn't answering the phone for Essence anymore her share was still sitting in an account. I was sitting in my office just enjoying life and for once I didn't feel lost, broken, and depressed. I must say meeting Honor and Thorne was the best thing for me.

"Ms. Sanchez...you have a delivery." My secretary Lola tapped on my office door.

"Come on in and put them on my desk."

"Ok...here you go and happy birthday." I looked at Lola and smiled. So, much had been going on and I had forgot all about my birthday until Thorne woke me up to a bunch of gifts. Then promised me a big dinner later tonight.

"Aww...thanks so much Lola, so much has been going on I actually forgot today was my birthday."

"Come on now Ms. Sanchez. You not that old to be forgetting your birthday. How old are you anyway?" Lola asked.

"I'm 20 years old today. I'm a little sad because this is my first year without my parents, but happy because I get to celebrate with my new family."

"Well...Ms. Sanchez let me tell you something. All the family I see working around here that you have. I'm sure you're going to have a wonderful birthday. Not to mention you deserve it. You've helped so many people since this place opened and I was one of them. So, hold your head high today and bask in your glory. Because baby you were put in this world to do some good and you're already doing it."

Lola came here a couple of months ago all scared and beaten. The pimp that she had ended up with had did a number on her and she was terrified. We took her in with open arms and then I had learned that she was once a secretary for a private law firm that she had gotten fired from for sleeping with the husband.

After she got fired her life spiraled out of control. To be honest she was one of the first clients we had taken in here at *"The Cinderella House."*

"Thank you so much Lola and I appreciate everything you do around here."

"Your welcome Ms. Sanchez." Lola said while heading out of the office until I stopped her.

"Lola...call me Rose please. Ms. Sanchez makes me sound all old." I said while winking at her. After Lola left, I opened up the card from the flowers and a smile crept up on my face.

My Love,

Today will be filled with all the things you love. Starting with lunch at the Grand Luxe Café. I'll pick you up around twelve. I love you lil' mama.

Your everything Thorne...

My life had turned upside down and I didn't think I would ever be able to get back after that. But having Thorne, Honor, Ms. Tina, Meagan, Essence, Cace, and Wiley in my life. Showed me that sometimes you have to go through sudden storms to have a perfect ending. I'm so happy with the way life is going and I plan to continue to help others find there happy ending.

Essence

I had been teaching at *"The Cinderella House"* for a couple of months now and I was enjoying every minute of it. I missed my mama a little, but not the way a daughter should. The person that I was really missing was Eboni. We didn't always see eye to eye but she still is my sister. I had just finished up a class. Now I was sitting in my office having lunch. My phone vibrated on my desk telling me I had a phone call coming through.

"Hello Essence Boyd, speaking...how can I help you?"

"Hello Mrs. Boyd, this is Dr. Shields calling from Cooper Hospital. We have an Eboni Boyd here. She was dropped off in the front of the hospital. She's fine and able to talk, but she looks as if she was beating. I know I wasn't supposed to call you because of doctor and patient privacy act. But when I looked up your name, I see you work at *"The Cinderella House."* It looks like she can benefit from a program like that, and ma'am she looks to be about four months pregnant."

"Ok...doctor thanks so much I'll be there in about ten minutes."

I hurried and hung my phone up and ran straight to Rose's office. I was scared, but I was happy that my sister finally had popped up. I had talked to her a few times but she would never tell me where she was. Rose said let her go and she would show up soon. I ran into Rose's office with tears in my eyes.

"What's wrong?" Rose ask while standing to her feet."

"We have to go to Cooper's they just called me. They have Eboni there."

"Oh My God...is she ok?",

"Yes, he said just beaten. He also said he wasn't supposed to call me but he saw in her information that I work here. He said he feels like she can benefit from what we got going on here. He also said she looks to be about four months pregnant."

"Wow...ok well come on. I'll have Meagan and Lola hold everything down until we get back. I'll also call Thorne to let him know. Did you call Wiley yet?" Rose asked.

"No...my nerves are all bad right now. Can you tell Thorne to tell him?"

Wiley and I had been dating for a little over four months. At first, he was a pain in the ass, but I grew to like him a lot. I actually think I'm falling for him already. He's showed me so much in the past couple of months it's crazy. Without him and Rose I wouldn't know where my head would be right now.

"Ok...I got you. Come on we can take my car, so you won't have to drive."

We ran out of the house in a hurry with everyone looking at us crazy. Rose left orders for Meagan and Lola to hold it down while we were gone. Honor would be there later as well so they should have been good.

Twenty minutes went by and we were now pulling up in the hospital parking lot. I hurried and jumped out and Rose followed behind me. I walked into the emergency room and flagged the first doctor I saw down.

"Hello...I'm looking for Eboni Boyd."

"Essence is that you?" I heard my sisters voice and I turned around to see where she was, and she came running straight to me. We both had our arms opened and we pulled each other in for a hug.

"I missed you so much. I tried to get away. I tried, but he wouldn't let me." Eboni cried while I held her.

"It's ok baby...it's ok you don't have to worry about whoever you're talking about anymore. Come on Rose and I have a place for you to go. We can get you cleaned up and you can tell me all about what happened."

"Baby you good?" The sound of Wiley's voice made me turn to see where he was. I looked at him and smiled. I then nodded my head letting him know that I was good. Thorne was holding Rose and I was holding Eboni and we all headed out of the hospital. I wasn't sure what the future held for me and my sister, but I indeed was looking forward to enjoying it. I had my career, my stepsister, my blood sister, and now my newly found love. Yeah, the puzzle to my life was just about complete.

Honor

The grand opening of *"Honor Thy Hair"* was last month and we've been nothing but busy. I loved everything about it. My life was so amazing of course I still was finishing up school being as though I started later then I was supposed to. So, I had to put the salon in Auntie Tina's name until I was finished school. Her, Rose, and Cace helped me find license stylist that could work in the shop. I didn't do hair in the shop just yet, but I still ran it. I did do hair and make up at the house that Rose ran. Some of the girls would come in so jacked up and feeling so insecure about themselves. I loved making them look beautiful again. I had just walked in **"The Cinderella House."** Rose had called me after her lunch that she had with Thorne to put me up on game. So, I knew I was coming in to do Eboni's hair. A name that I was shocked to hear, since she had been MIA. I sat my things in Rose's office and made my way to the salon part that was in the house. Rose and Thorne hooked this place up it looked nothing like it did when it was just a regular house. I was so amazed at how fast we got it up and running. When Rose first came to me with the idea, I looked at her and thought this girl was heaven sent. After all she just went through all she was concerned about was helping others.

"Hey...Eboni it's nice to see you." I said walking into the salon.

"Hello Honor, how are you?"

"I'm fine just living. What can I do for you today?"

"I don't know just make me look good. I'm going to Rose's dinner tonight and I can't be showing up around people with a black eye." She giggled.

I didn't know what to say to that. I just went along with the punches. It always amazed me how Rose even still dealt with them. After the shit they watched their mother do to her, but to each is own. I know if it was me, I wouldn't be able to trust them fully.

"Ok...well you can come sit in my chair." When Eboni got up, I noticed her little belly which caused a smile on my face.

"I was thinking a up type do, and it's been a minute since I washed my hair. So, I did it while I was in the shower when I first got here."

"Alright...that's fine. How many months are you? If you don't mind me asking."

"No, I don't mind you asking. I'm four months, and Honor I know we always had words in school, but you don't have to worry about that anymore. I had a lot of issues back then. Some I have dealt with and some I still need help with, but I'm going to try my best to change my ways for the better. I have a little person to live for."

"It's going to take me some getting use to so please bear with me. Usually if I don't fuck with you then I don't fuck with you, but my bestie loves her stepsisters no matter what. So, I'll definitely try for her." I said truthfully Rose really did love them and if she was going to deal with them then I would keep it cordial.

"Yes, and we love Rose too. At first, I was angry with her, but then when I heard all the bad stuff my mama did it shocked the hell out of me. Which is why I needed my space, but that caused me to be homeless then I met up with a guy that got me off the streets. I thought he loved me, but he turned out to be a fucking monster."

"So, how did you get away?"

"He owed some dude money and they broke into the house. They let me go as long as I promised not to rat them out. Shit that nigga had just beat my ass. I didn't say shit, I left right out of the door. Hitchhiked a ride and had the driver drop me off at the hospital."

"Oh My God...well I'm glad you're ok and your sister has been worried sick about you."

"I know and I'm glad I made it back to her because it was nights I got beaten so bad. I thought I was never going to see her ever again.

The smell of my man walking into the salon caught my attention. I walked up to him and pulled him in for a hug before he even came all the way inside.

"Hey baby... I bought your clothes so you can get dressed here. You said you had three heads and you didn't wanna be late for Rose's dinner." Cace said.

"Yeah...I don't wanna be late. I thought you had some work to do at the sneaker store?"

"Baby I'm the boss I made somebody else do it." Cace chuckled.

Cace had seen everyone around him opening up they own business and he wanted to do the same. He told me that he didn't wanna be in the streets for ever so why not have something to fall back on. When we decided to make a family. We had a pregnancy scare right after I got shot. I hadn't been taking my birth control. So, since I wanted to wait until I was twenty-three to have kids, we decided on me doing the IUD for birth control. It stays in for five years, so hopefully when I take it out, we'll be married and ready to start making babies. So, life was going great for your girl and Cace was the best man a girl could ask for. I saw him and only him in my future, we were the next power couple making moves and making sure we paved the way for our future family.

Thorne

"So, you think you ready to do this?" Cace asked while walking into the men's bathroom at Ruth's Chris Steak House. I decided to take the whole family out to dinner then we were going to head the Penn's Landing to take late night engagement pictures. Yeah y'all heard right today was my baby's birthday and I was ready to pop the question.

"Nigga of course I'm ready. Rose is my world." I smiled while thinking about when I first met her. She was so broken, but I knew she was going to be just right for me.

"I'm just asking to make sure."

"Why would you even ask some shit like that?" Wiley asked while shaking his head.

Life had been great lately. Business was flowing in every end. Me and my family were straight and safe. Since we got all the bad seeds out the way. Now I was working hard to build some other projects so one day I could leave this street shit alone period. My boys were thinking the same which is why we were training a couple of our best men to take over. I first I felt some type of way about letting go of Big Russ' legacy. Until Rose told me that I needed to make my own legacy and do my own shit, so I'll have something to tell our children when we have some.

"Alright y'all we've been in this bathroom forever like the ladies not waiting on us." I said.

"What they rushing us for? Everybody ate already." Wiley said.

"I know, but they don't wanna bring the cake out until we back to the table." Cace said.

We walked out of the bathroom and headed to the table. The waiter looked at me and I gave him a head nod to bring the cake out. Once I gave him the ok all the waiters came out singing happy birthday along with the other guest in the restaurant. Once the song was finished everyone around the table started giving speeches with a toast letting Rose know how much she meant to them. That alone had me ready to pop the question. At first, she was shy and quiet, but when you get to know her little ass she was too much. *I laughed at my thoughts*. I banged my fork on the side of my glass, so I could get everyone to quiet down.

"Since everyone said there little speeches, I believe it's time for mine. What I wanna start off with is letting you know that you definitely complete me. At first when I first laid eyes on you it was something inside of me that made me wanna help you. I could tell you had some shit going on in your head and I honestly wanted to help. Not knowing I was going to fall for you as hard and fast as I did. Everyone noticed the good in you just by meeting you one time. Even my mama, I got threatened by her numerous times telling me that I better treat you the way you deserve to be treated or leave you the hell alone. I promised her that you were it for me and I wanted no one but you. Of course, she didn't believe me until a couple of months ago when I came to talk to her. I thought you were going to leave my black ass because of that Kreesha situation and I went crying to my mama like a little bitch. I said all this to say." I managed to get out while the sweat ran down my forehead. I got on one knee and everyone started screaming and Rose started crying.

"Thorne what are you doing down there?" Rose asked while the tears fell from her eyes.

"I said all that to say...baby you're it for me and I want you to be my wife. Rose will you marry me?" I asked and everyone screamed and jumped up and down.

"Yes...Thorne...Yes...I'll marry you." Rose yelled out while standing and pulling me off the floor and in for a hug. She pulled my face to hers then kissed me passionately.

"I love you so much Mr. Williams."

"I love you more Mrs. Williams." I knew we were both young but we were old enough to know how we felt about each other. Besides I wasn't taking no for an answer Rose Sanchez was always going to be my wife from the very first moment I laid eyes on her.

A Thorne defends the Rose, harming only those who would try to steal the blossom.

The end...

CPSIA information can be obtained
at www.ICGtesting.com
Printed in the USA
LVHW111515011119
636084LV00002B/199/P

9 781689 439374